Catscape

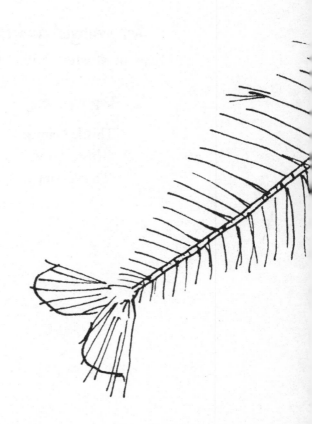

To Niamh

Catscape

Mike Nicholson

Happy reading!

Mike Nicholson

Kelpies

Kelpies is an imprint of Floris Books

Published in 2005 by Floris Books
Fifth printing 2017
© 2005 Mike Nicholson

The publisher acknowledges subsidy from
Creative Scotland towards the publication
of this volume

 This book is also
available as an eBook

British Library CIP Data available
ISBN 978-086315-531-4
Printed by TJ International

To Joy and Joseph for the great times we've had together in Comely Bank

My thanks to all the family, friends and the writing group, Broadside, who encouraged me along the way.

1. A Time-keeping Problem

Ever since he had first looked in the window of Crockett's Watches and Clocks, Fergus Speight had known exactly what he wanted for his twelfth birthday. Looking beyond the carriage clocks and the padded velvet trays of shiny silver watches, Fergus's gaze had come to an abrupt halt on the display of digital watches. Each of the watches had blinked at him as they counted time, but one in particular had caught his eye. It was spinning slowly around on its own little podium and a tiny plaque at the bottom declared that this was "The DataBoy." A small card alongside proudly proclaimed that the DataBoy was "One Funky Watch with Twenty Funky Functions," while a list below showed that these included a stopwatch, calculator, thermometer, light and a display of times in twenty-five countries around the world ... and those were only the first five.

Since then, Fergus had tried to pass Crockett's as often as he could. Each time he reversed his baseball cap so that he could get close enough to the window to see which of the DataBoy's functions was on show. The previous week, one of the shop assistants had come outside to say that Mr. Crockett would prefer it if Fergus didn't stand quite so close to the window, because he was steaming it up for the other customers.

With his birthday fast approaching, Fergus was pretty sure that his mum would get the DataBoy for him, but had decided not to say anything until she asked him what he wanted. He was basing this tactic on a particularly hard lesson he had learned on his last birthday. A year ago he had asked her so often for a DVD called "The Pyramid Maze" that she did buy it for him, but also removed the plug from the DVD player so that he couldn't watch it for three long days.

It seemed to take forever between Fergus's first view of the DataBoy and Mrs. Speight asking him about his birthday. However, when she finally did they happened to be on Raeburn Place quite close to Crockett's Watches and Clocks. Without a word, Fergus had taken his mum firmly by her coat sleeve, and had pulled her towards the shop window, narrowly avoiding a pedestrian pile-up with a dog, a woman with a pushchair and an old man with a walking stick, in his rush to get there.

"Are you quite sure that's what you want?' said his mum, smiling as she looked through the glass at the DataBoy while she tried to return her coat to its original shape.

"It does so many things!" Fergus said excitely, "Twenty Funky Functions!"

"Is one of them tidying bedrooms?" his mum asked, leaning towards the window to read the information on the DataBoy.

"I could find out for you," replied Fergus hopefully.

So when the morning of Fergus's birthday arrived, just at the start of the summer holidays, it was no surprise that one of his presents was a long, slim rectangular package in shiny silver paper, about the length of a watch and strap. Fergus tore into the paper excitedly and opened the box to reveal the DataBoy, then spent most of the day staring at the gleaming watch on his wrist and testing all the functions. He checked the temperature inside and outside the flat using the thermometer, added up the items on an old till receipt on the calculator, and found out the time differences between Rio de Janeiro and Tokyo.

The day after his birthday, Fergus was still finding ways to make use of his new watch. He and his mum had just been to the shops on Raeburn Place and were heading home with two bags of groceries. As they turned into Comely Bank Avenue, Fergus decided to time how long it would take to get from the traffic lights to their flat at number 81. He was concentrating so hard on the DataBoy as they walked, that he didn't anticipate the horror that was rapidly approaching until he happened to glance up.

Blue shoes, blue stockings, blue coat, blue scarf, blue hat and even a hint of blue in the steely grey hair underneath ... Mrs. Scrimgeour was coming towards them.

Fergus immediately tugged at his mum's coat, whispering, "Cross the road ... quick!"

"Fergus, don't be so rude," said his mum who was clearly also trying to work out if dodging the traffic was worth the risk to avoid meeting Mrs. Scrimgeour.

Fergus groaned, knowing from previous experience that an encounter with Mrs. Scrimgeour would mean being trapped in a one-sided conversation for at least fifteen minutes. As Mrs. Scrimgeour spotted them she let out a loud "YOO HOO!" Fergus felt that he was about to be enveloped by a large blue cloud from which there was no escape.

"FIONA, FERGUS, LOVELY TO SEE YOU," bellowed Mrs. Scrimgeour.

"Lovely to see you too, Beryl," said Mrs. Speight.

Fergus switched off as Mrs. Scrimgeour launched into conversation, beginning most of her sentences with "AND HAVE YOU HEARD ABOUT THE PEOPLE AT NUMBER ...?"

He decided to continue to put his new watch to practical use by timing how long Mrs. Scrimgeour could speak without taking a breath. It was 11.33 am when he began counting the seconds. After a few goes, Fergus gave up, reaching the conclusion that Mrs. Scrimgeour must be like a frog and breathe through her skin, because as hard as he tried he couldn't spot any gaps between the words when she might be drawing breath.

As his mum stood listening and nodding patiently while Mrs. Scrimgeour droned on, Fergus began pushing a small stone around with the edge of his trainer. He moved it onto a metal manhole cover, and began nudging the stone backwards and forwards along its grooves. "Maybe by the time I get to the other side of the cover they'll be finished," he thought.

It soon became a race for Fergus to get the stone across the grooves when he heard his mum say, "We really have to get going now," for what he thought was the fourteenth time, although he had lost count somewhere around seven.

"At last!" whispered Fergus, as they broke free and headed up the last bit of Comely Bank Avenue.

"She could talk the hind legs off a donkey," said his mum.

Fergus decided that if this was true, Mrs. Scrimgeour probably had a large collection of donkey legs stuffed and mounted in glass cases around her house.

Fergus and his mum continued up the road until they reached number 81, where Fergus checked his watch again.

"No way!" he shouted.

"Fergus!" his mother said sternly as she put her key in the lock. "Don't shout!"

"My watch isn't working!" wailed Fergus.

Sure enough the DataBoy was showing the time as 11.26. It had lost seven minutes since he had last looked at it. Mrs. Speight glanced at the digital figures, and spotting the seconds ticking over said, "Well it seems to be working now. Isn't it just a little slow?"

"But it was 11.33 a minute ago," said Fergus.

"That doesn't make sense. I know that it did feel as if time was standing still when I was listening to Mrs. Scrimgeour but I didn't realize it was going backwards!" said his mum, laughing at her own joke. Fergus didn't find this funny, considering the seriousness of his brand new watch being broken.

"Come on," his mum said, "we'll re-set your watch and see how it goes. If there's a problem we can always take it back to Mr. Crockett. In the meantime why don't you use it to see how quickly we can put the shopping away?"

Throughout the rest of the day, Fergus looked at his watch just as much as before, although each glance was now with some suspicion as he checked closely to see if it was working like a new DataBoy should. All of the functions performed perfectly over the following few days and so Fergus began to forget about his new watch going backwards. Until … it happened again!

A week later, Fergus was heading down Comely Bank Avenue towards the corner shop, clutching a short list of things that his mum had asked him to get. Just before he got to the shop, he passed a lamppost, with a homemade poster tied loosely to it, fluttering in the breeze. He glanced at it as he wandered past and had gone a few more paces before the words sank in; "Reward, Lost cat. Black and white. Called Rainbow."

"A black and white cat called Rainbow?" thought Fergus. "Someone has a great sense of humour." He slowly registered that there was some other writing on the poster and backtracked to look more closely. In typed print under the cat's description it said "£10 reward for information. £40 for safe return."

"Wow, that would be useful money," thought Fergus, not needing the calculator on his DataBoy to work out that £40 could mean a few CDs or a few weeks' worth of sweets. At the bottom of the poster was a contact phone number. Fergus went into the corner shop to ask George, the shopkeeper, if he could borrow a pen and paper to take a note of it. He nipped back outside, wrote down the details and made up his mind to keep an eye out for a black and white cat called Rainbow.

After buying the milk, magazine and onions on his mum's list, Fergus said goodbye to George and headed home. Outside the shop he noticed another "Reward" poster, this time stuck to a postbox.

"£25 reward for the return of a Tabby cat called Tabby," it declared. Fergus couldn't help wondering what he would call a cat if he had one, but decided that Tabby and Rainbow would be fairly low on his list.

He went back to the shop to borrow the pen again. "I should start charging for this," said George. "How about 10p for every word? Does that seem reasonable?" Fergus said that he would be happy to negotiate if he got one of the rewards.

Fergus set off for home for a second time, passing the manhole cover where he had been kicking the stone the previous week. Distracted from thoughts of lost cats and reward money, Fergus remembered that timing his journey home that day had been interrupted by Mrs. Scrimgeour. Deciding to have another go, he stood on the metal cover and set the stopwatch on his DataBoy. Suddenly Fergus blinked hard and stared at the watch. Surely he must be imagining things? He could have sworn that it had just jumped back a minute. Had it really just gone from 10.47 to 10.46? He stared even harder at his watch, trying desperately not to blink and break his concentration. Then after a minute had passed he saw what he had been waiting for. His watch changed to 10.45.

Something made Fergus look down at his feet. Was it

just a coincidence that his watch had lost time twice when he had been standing on the same spot? The manhole cover he was standing on looked as normal as any other that he seen before, although Fergus knew that he couldn't claim to be an expert in this field. As he bent down to look more closely he was unprepared for what happened next. Out of the corner of his eye he saw a movement just before impact occurred, and the next things he saw were the sky and his baseball cap flying past. Not realizing that he had been knocked off his feet and had whacked his head on the pavement he couldn't work out why his left cheek was getting a big wet stripe on it every two seconds. Opening his eyes he found that a small white dog was licking his face enthusiastically.

Fergus heard somebody say, "Heel, Jock, heel!" Looking round blearily from his prone position he saw a rather round boy standing a few feet away holding a Metro scooter, which Fergus reckoned must have been going at top speed until a few seconds before. The dog was now panting heavily beside the boy's scruffy baseball boots. The boy was carrying a small but very heavy-looking rucksack and seemed to have come out of the incident remarkably unharmed.

"Sorry, I didn't see you," he said, scratching his head and looking a bit embarrassed.

"That's good news," said Fergus sitting up and brushing down his combats. "I'd hate to think it was deliberate." The boy grinned sheepishly beneath a mop of curly brown hair. "My name's Murdo and you've just met Jock," he said pointing at the small Jack Russell. "What's your name?"

"Fergus," said Fergus, getting shakily to his feet, rubbing his short blond hair and finding to his surprise that he was not bleeding from anywhere. He picked up his baseball cap and it was then that he noticed Murdo's bulging rucksack in more detail. There was equipment popping out of every pocket — a pair of headphones, a clipboard, a torch and pens attached to every available flap.

"What's all that stuff?" Fergus asked. Murdo looked a bit embarrassed.

"Oh just some bits and pieces I use," he said sounding like he wanted to avoid the subject. "What were you doing on that manhole cover anyway?"

"I ... I was about to time how long it took me to walk home from there," Fergus said unconvincingly. Murdo looked slightly puzzled by this explanation, but didn't say anything.

At that moment Fergus realized that in the crash, he had not only dropped his small bag of shopping, but his piece of paper with the details of the lost cats was also blowing away down the street. Spotting the problem, Murdo nipped over on his scooter and slapped the paper down with his foot. Picking it up and looking at Fergus's scribbles he said cautiously, "Are you looking for the cats as well?"

"Ummm ... well I thought I might have a go," said Fergus.

"You've only got two on your list," said Murdo, trying to smooth out Fergus's rather crumpled piece of paper.

"I only copied them down five minutes ago," said Fergus defensively, wondering about Murdo's line of questioning. "Have *you* got a list?" Murdo hesitated, looked around as if to see if anyone else was watching, and then took off his rucksack and unbuckled the top. He pulled out a loose-leaf folder, which had bits of paper almost fighting each other to get out. Squatting on the pavement, he opened it, flicked through the well-thumbed pages and looked up smiling. Each page was a photocopy of a different lost cat poster. Fergus's eyes widened.

"Wow ... there must be about forty there!" he said. Murdo looked impressed.

"Forty-three actually," he replied.

"Have you been collecting them over the years?" said Fergus.

"No, that's just it," said Murdo, the excitement rising in his voice. "These are all from the last three months and all from within two miles of here!"

Fergus eyes widened still further. He then started putting two and two together and began to come up with a very large number. "How much do all the rewards add up to?" he said trying not to sound too interested. Murdo pointed to a list on the inside cover of his folder which had every cat's name and a number beside each entry. "£750 and five more which promise 'a substantial reward,'" said Murdo with a gleam in his eye.

"Wow! ... and have you found any of the cats so far?" he asked, squatting beside Murdo and slowly turning over the pages in the folder.

"Not a single one. These cats have just disappeared into thin air," said Murdo. "Listen, why don't we go for a coke and I'll fill you in? I've been dying to tell someone about all this for ages."

An hour later, having delivered some bruised onions, dented milk, a crumpled magazine and a hurried explanation to his mother, Fergus was perched on a window seat in the Copper Kettle Café on Raeburn Place. His head was reeling but it was no longer a result of being upended by Murdo. He was now trying to come to terms with information on cats of every name and description. At the same time his stomach was spinning in a different direction with the after-effects of two cokes, two doughnuts and a vanilla slice.

Murdo had been on "the case," as he kept calling it, for three months, initially spending time at weekends, but now using every day of the summer holidays to try and make some progress in finding even one of the missing cats. He had certainly been very busy. He had visited all forty-three "lost cat owners" and had recorded descriptions of their cats and details of where and when their cats had gone missing.

Murdo kept mentioning his "Incident Room," which he described as the "nerve centre" of his lost-cat operation. Fergus was already excited at the idea of trying to solve what seemed like an intriguing mystery, and had agreed to visit Murdo's Incident Room at the earliest opportunity.

"What's the time?" asked Murdo. "I think I'd better be getting home." Fergus pulled up his sleeve.

"That's a DataBoy!" said Murdo, his eyes widening.

Before Fergus could say anything, Murdo disappeared off his seat and started rummaging in one of his rucksack's many pockets. A moment later he pulled out a rather scratched looking DataBoy, which had only one piece of its strap attached. "They're brilliant, aren't they?" he said flourishing his watch. "This hasn't lost a second in ten months, even though I've given it a bit of a hard time," he said ruefully looking at the missing strap and chipped glass. Fergus realized that he had been so absorbed in the story of Murdo's investigations that he had quite forgotten about his watch's timekeeping problems.

"I didn't tell you why I was looking at that manhole cover," Fergus said, making a snap decision that Murdo might be someone who would believe his curious story. Sure enough, Murdo listened intently as Fergus described how his new watch had developed a curious habit of going backwards.

"Well there's only one thing to do," said Murdo. "Let's go and test my DataBoy in the same place!"

Fergus grinned and without delay the boys paid up, collected Jock from outside and headed back to the scene of their collision.

2. The Incident Room

"It's been a strange day," thought Fergus as he followed Murdo Fraser and Jock through the streets away from Comely Bank Avenue. It was unusual enough to collide with someone who then becomes your enthusiastic new friend, but to discover that the city's cats were mysteriously disappearing really took the biscuit. However, the biscuit had not only been taken but scoffed in one great gulp, as Fergus had watched Murdo stand on the manhole cover only to see his older, and supposedly reliable, DataBoy blink backwards through the minutes. Murdo had shaken his head in disbelief and had then systematically stood on a range of paving slabs around the manhole cover but was unable to repeat the strange effect. Fergus was secretly pleased to find that if he was going completely mad then at least he had Murdo for company. Meanwhile, Murdo had been more than a little upset to find that what he described as "the best watch I've ever had" now had a tendency to go in the wrong direction.

The boys got some curious glances from passers-by as they stood staring at their watches at various points on the pavement or at the edge of the road. Jock looked on in an equally quizzical manner, with his head cocked to one side. They found nothing strange until they stood on the manhole cover. Every time they did that, their watches went very slowly, but very definitely, into reverse. Murdo finally concluded that going back to the Incident Room to work out a plan was the only way to think about missing cats and backwards watches. A quick visit to Mrs. Speight cleared Fergus to go to Murdo's for a couple of hours without having to give much away about the two mysteries they were intent on solving.

Now, as the boys turned into 101, Orchard Brae Gardens, Murdo announced that they had arrived. Although bordered by neat flowerbeds on either side there was no way to stand back and admire the front garden because taking up most of the driveway was a small caravan.

"This is the Incident Room," said Murdo proudly. "Dad keeps saying he's going to sell it because we never take it anywhere, but in the meantime I've commandeered it for the investigation."

Producing a bunch of keys from his pocket and looking over either shoulder as if there was someone watching them, he unlocked the caravan's door and entered. Jock slipped in under his feet as Fergus glanced back to the road. There was no sign of anyone at all on Orchard Brae Gardens, and he wondered if Murdo wasn't taking his investigations just a little too seriously.

Not quite knowing what to expect, Fergus entered the caravan. Even though it was the middle of a sunny summer day, it was gloomy inside as the blinds were pulled down and the curtains closed. Murdo switched on a lamp in one corner and Fergus began to take in the scene.

He had already had hints of the organization behind Murdo's efforts to find the cats, but nothing had prepared Fergus for the inside of the Incident Room.

On the left-hand wall was a huge map of Edinburgh dotted with a multicoloured rash of map pins. Each had a thread leading out towards a numbered flag, giving the effect of a giant spider's web across the city. Fergus could see numbers going into the forties and realized that each flag corresponded to the home of a missing cat.

"Forty-three cats and a pin for every one," said Murdo noticing Fergus looking at the map. "The pins show where the owners live, which was usually the last place that their cat was seen."

"Over there is my filing system with all the investigation documents." He pointed to three grey metal cabinets, each of which had drawers marked with big white labels boasting Murdo's alphabetical filing system in red marker pen from A to Z.

"These are my reference texts," said Murdo moving round the small caravan and waving grandly at two shelves bending under the weight of all the folders and books stacked on them. At a first glance Fergus could see various maps and guides to Edinburgh, an *Encyclopaedia of Cats,* and a book called *Cats are from Mars and Dogs are from Venus.* On the table in the middle of the caravan sat a set of desk trays marked "In," "Pending" and "For Filing." The "For Filing" tray was empty and Fergus reckoned this was yet another indication of Murdo's organizational abilities. Another sign was the thick hardback notebook, which Murdo handed to Fergus. The sticker on the front said "Investigation Diary." Inside it neatly listed every activity that Murdo had undertaken as part of his attempts to locate the cats. "I write it up each night," he said, with a glint of pride in his eyes.

"This is amazing," said Fergus as he gazed around the caravan and leafed through the diary.

"Well, these cats have certainly kept me busy," said Murdo sounding very serious, as he watched Fergus's reaction with pleasure.

"Right," Murdo said grabbing a red marker pen and heading for the large whiteboard which took up most of one wall. "It's time to have some fresh ideas on the case."

To Fergus it looked as though every idea that Murdo had ever had was written neatly on it already, but wiping a corner clean with a cloth, Murdo stood poised for action.

"Come on, we need to brainstorm," he said, his pen poised at the board.

"What does that mean?" asked Fergus.

"It's ... it's ... it's what you do ... you know ... for ideas ... word association, no holds barred. We need blue sky thinking, Fergus!"

Murdo was waving his arms around enthusiastically as he spoke but Fergus could honestly say he hadn't a clue what his new friend was talking about. He wondered if Murdo actually had much of an idea himself, but decided that it didn't really matter because it was certainly entertaining.

Murdo stopped waving his arms and prepared to write on the board again. "If I said 'cats' what words do you think of?"

"Meow," said Fergus giving his best cat impersonation.

Jock barked loudly from his basket in the corner and settled down again.

"Good," said Murdo writing 'Meow' on the board. "Come on, what else?"

"Kitten, ball of wool, stuck in trees ... firemen?" said Fergus.

"Excellent, excellent," said Murdo enthusiastically, writing as fast as he could, his tongue sticking out of the corner of his mouth as he concentrated on getting all of Fergus's suggestions written on the board. "Keep going. Remember, think big!"

"You mean like lions, tigers, leopards?" said Fergus.

"No ... no ... no ... pet cats ... but think differently ... think ... think out of the box!"

Fergus wasn't sure which box he was supposed to think out of, but gave it a go.

"Whiskers. Eating fish ... er ... I'm getting stuck now," said Fergus.

"Right, we'll move on then," said Murdo in a business-like manner. He drew a line under Fergus's suggestions. "What if I said the word 'lost?'"

"Lost ..." said Fergus pondering on the word. "What about missing, gone, disappeared ... runaway, stolen ... kidnapped ... catnapped?"

"Slow down, slow down ..." said Murdo, squeaking the big marker pen over the board and spelling 'kidnapped' with only one 'p.' Fergus weighed up whether he should point this out, but decided that Murdo would *not* appreciate the interruption.

"Now," said Murdo standing back and looking at his work, "do any of these help us?"

"Well, it's obvious," said Fergus. "We need to look for a fireman with a giant ball of wool who is encouraging cats to run away from home."

"If you're not going to take this seriously then you might as well go," said Murdo huffily, looking at the writing on the board but not coming up with any alternative suggestions.

"Sorry," said Fergus. "Well, cats don't get lost do they? And not that many of them would run away ... so from our list that leaves us with them being stolen. But why would anyone steal cats?"

"To sell them somewhere?" said Murdo.

"To set up a cat zoo?" Murdo gave Fergus a warning look that suggested he wasn't being serious enough again.

At that moment there was a knock at the door.

"Who is it?" said Murdo.

"The Prime Minister of Swaziland," said a girl's voice.

"What's the password?" said Murdo curtly.

"Your heid's mince," said the voice. Fergus stifled a smile.

"Incorrect," said Murdo, looking flustered.

"Oh come on, Murdo, you know it's me," said the girl's voice.

"That's not the point, it's security," said Murdo stiffly. Fergus was curious to see who was giving Murdo a difficult time and at that moment the door opened.

"Yeah, that's really secure," said the girl stepping boldly into the caravan, seemingly without a care, and certainly without Murdo's invitation to do so. Fergus guessed that the girl was a good two or three years older than him and Murdo, had a mischievous smile on her face and was looking around the Incident Room as if to find something new to make fun of. The only new thing was the arrival of Fergus.

"Hallo," she said spotting Fergus, "I'm Heather ... Murdo's loving sister." She gave a pretend sickly smile and leered towards Murdo as she said this.

"Hi," said Fergus weakly, feeling slightly uncomfortable at the girl's confidence and completely forgetting to introduce himself in return.

"You must be Dr. Watson," said Heather, continuing to address him and ignoring Murdo.

Fergus felt confused and could only manage to say "Er ... um," rather than anything intelligent in response. Heather's eyes rolled upwards in exasperation. "You must be Dr. Watson because he thinks he's Sherlock Holmes," she said spelling it out carefully and pointing towards Murdo. "You'll need to be a bit quicker than that if you're going to solve any mysteries," she added.

"What do you want?" said Murdo. A sullen expression had replaced his previous enthusiasm as soon as Heather had breezed into his "secure zone."

"Have you got any batteries? I need some for my discman," said Heather, looking around the caravan, trying to spot what she wanted.

Suddenly her face changed. Looking over Murdo's left shoulder her eyes widened. She gasped and pointed, "Murdo ... behind you ... a CAT!"

Murdo spun round. As he did so, Heather grabbed a new packet of batteries from the table top and with a laugh jumped back out of the caravan, leaving the door flapping open as a final insult to Murdo's security precautions.

Murdo was red in the face, and Fergus wasn't quite sure where to look for a few moments. "She seems nice," he said, trying to break the silence.

Murdo walked over stiffly and shut the door. "She is impossible — how can I be expected to work under these conditions?" he said, tight-lipped with anger. He turned back to the whiteboard and shook his head violently as if to rid himself of any memory of Heather's intrusion. "Now where were we?"

There was another knock at the door.

"Go A-WAY," said Murdo.

"That's charming," said a woman's voice.

"Oops, sorry, Mum," said Murdo instantly changing his tone. "Em, ... password please."

"It's your mother," said the woman opening the door, "I don't need a password."

Fergus concluded that Murdo really needed a review of his security systems. Murdo meanwhile just stood shaking his head slowly and sadly, as if wondering where it had all gone wrong.

Murdo's mother, Mrs. Fraser, stood in the doorway, "Heather told me you had company, Murdo. I just wondered if you boys wanted some lunch ... but I would need an introduction first," she added, turning and smiling at Fergus.

Murdo introduced Fergus and within ten minutes the boys were sitting at the kitchen table in the house, with steaming bowls of soup and crusty bread in front of them. Mrs. Fraser asked Fergus lots of questions about what he liked doing, where he lived and who he lived with, and he soon began to relax and feel really at home.

Meanwhile, after the security breaches, Murdo seemed to have regained some of his earlier enthusiasm. His mum knew a little bit about his efforts to find the cats and Fergus was amused to hear himself being described as a "colleague working in the same field." Fergus did notice that he didn't mention the curious mystery of the DataBoys, however, and began to wonder if Murdo wasn't really that interested in the malfunctioning watches. However, he was proved wrong when Mrs. Fraser left the room for a few moments and Murdo leant towards him with a determined whisper.

"I've been thinking. We can't just concentrate on the cats. We need to move things along with the watch investigation too. I don't know how we can do it but we have to find out what's underneath that manhole cover. Any ideas?"

Before Fergus could answer, Mrs. Fraser came back into the room and Murdo instantly picked up where he had left off about the missing cats. "So we really need to get back and plan our next moves on the case, Mum. Can we go?"

Mrs. Fraser had a smile on her face that revealed years of listening patiently to Murdo. "Murdo wants to go, but I have the power to make him stay with just two words," she said looking at Fergus. Fergus smiled back and waited to see Mrs. Fraser work her magic words.

By now Murdo was sidling out of his seat. "Mum, we've got work to do!" he said impatiently.

"Sponge pudding," said Mrs. Fraser.

Murdo stopped in his tracks and his round face changed to a combination of pleasure at the thought of his favourite dessert and sadness that his mother had got the better of him once again.

"I'll get the syrup," he said, changing direction to fetch a chair so he could reach up to a cupboard. He plonked a tin on the table and pulled a teaspoon from a nearby drawer. Sticking the end of the spoon's handle under the edge of the lid, Murdo worked his way around it and prised it open to reveal the sticky smooth golden contents.

By now, Mrs. Fraser had put a bowl with a steaming chunk of sponge pudding in front of each of the boys, and with a well-practised twirl of the teaspoon, Murdo transferred a big glob of syrup from the tin to trickle on to his piece of sponge.

Fergus found himself staring at the tin or, to be more precise, at the lid, which was now upside down on the table with the teaspoon beside it. A lever and a lid — it was so easy. He looked up at Murdo who was halfway through his pudding already.

"I've got the answer to your question," said Fergus.

"What question?" said Murdo through a mouthful of syrupy sponge.

"You asked if I had any ideas," said Fergus putting the lid back on the tin and then prising it off again with the end of the spoon. He tapped his DataBoy to show Murdo that the mystery of the manhole cover and the watches might be solved with some simple levering. Murdo's eyes widened and he nodded quickly. Furiously spooning sponge pudding into his mouth he spoke through sticky teeth. "Eat up, we've got some calculations to do."

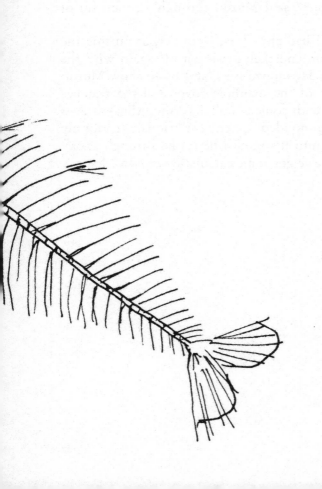

3. Under Cover

After just a few hours Fergus was getting the hang of the way that Murdo Fraser worked. It reminded him of last year's Guy Fawkes Night. Fergus had looked at the fireworks at a neighbour's bonfire party, and remembered liking the instructions — "light blue touch-paper and stand well back." This seemed to be a similar instruction to give to anyone who was going to spend some time with Murdo. To activate him, you just had to put a small idea in his head and then get out of the way as he exploded into action, usually in different directions at the same time. Fergus concluded that "standing well back" might not be enough in Murdo's case. The warning should probably read "dive for cover." The mere suggestion of prising open the manhole cover had sent Murdo into a frenzy in the Incident Room. The problem with the Incident Room was that it wasn't big enough for frenzies, or for anyone to "stand well back" in. To complicate matters, Jock got involved in Murdo's bouts of activity, scrambling around under his feet and barking in what he thought was a helpful fashion.

Murdo began by wanting to estimate the size and weight of the manhole cover. Fergus was prepared to take an educated guess, but that was not enough for Murdo. The process for him involved drawings, a measuring tape, a calculator, a set of kitchen scales, a number of heavy books and the lid of a casserole dish. Fergus didn't think that Mrs. Fraser would have been too impressed with her kitchen equipment being used as a pretend manhole cover. If you added the fact that the boys were planning to have a look under the pavement of Comely Bank Avenue at night when they were supposed to be asleep, Fergus felt sure that Mr. Fraser would close the Incident Room down and sell it off in a flash.

Fortunately, Mrs. Fraser remained oblivious to the boys' activities and despite his complicated calculations Murdo reached the conclusion that the manhole cover was "probably quite heavy."

"Very useful, but what could we actually use to lift it up?" asked Fergus. With that Murdo was off again as Fergus continued to be an amused spectator. First there was a fruitless search in the garden shed before they moved on to the garage where Murdo's dad had a workbench, with a variety of tools.

"I'm not supposed to fiddle about with this stuff," said Murdo beginning to fiddle about with the stuff. After weighing up various hammers, the largest screwdriver Fergus had ever seen, and drill bits of every length and thickness, Murdo went headfirst into a cupboard and began rummaging around with only his bottom and pudgy legs on show. A few minutes later there was a muffled, but enormous "Ah-ha!"

He emerged red-faced, sweating and triumphantly clutching a crowbar. "This is what we're after," said Murdo. "I've never seen Dad use this so there's no way he'll miss it for a night."

Fergus and Murdo replaced all the other tools to cover their tracks and returned to the Incident Room for the next stage of the planning. Using the crowbar they practised lifting the pile of books and the casserole lid.

"Right," said Murdo brandishing the crowbar happily. "We now have the technology to open the cover."

"If we do manage to lift the manhole cover," said Fergus, "what do we do next?"

"Just have a look," said Murdo with a vague wave of his hand. "How can we plan when we don't know what we'll find?"

"Well we need to think it through a bit further, otherwise it will be a bit of a waste of time," explained Fergus. "For a start we'll need a torch." Thirty seconds later a big torch had joined their growing pile of equipment on the table.

"Do you think ...? Would we ...? Would we actually go down there?" said Murdo trying to hide his rising concern with this project by asking an innocent question.

Fergus thought this through. He was beginning to realize that the fun of planning the expedition was now reaching the point where they had to decide exactly how much they were prepared to do.

"I think that might be a bit risky," he said. "I think at this stage it's just a ... a ... preliminary investigation."

"That sounds good," said Murdo. "I like that." He seemed relieved.

"Although it would be a bit disappointing if the torch didn't shine far enough and we didn't see anything," continued Fergus. "We'd be none the wiser. We'd be back to square one."

There was silence as the boys pondered the situation.

"What if we could hear?" said Fergus thinking aloud.

Once again Murdo sprang into action, emerging with an old and rather bulky walkman.

"If I remember rightly this has a 'record' function on it," he said, inserting a tape and attaching a tiny microphone lead to it. "Testing, testing — one, two, three," he said rather pompously before replaying it to confirm that it was working. "Excellent," he said adding it to the pile of equipment.

"Problem," said Fergus.

"What?" said Murdo looking confused.

"Well the lead isn't that long," said Fergus, "It won't even go down as far as we can see with the torch."

Five minutes later the collection of equipment included a large ball of string.

"Are we getting there?" asked Murdo. "Crowbar if it's

heavy, torch if it's too dark, microphone if we can't see, string if it's too deep," he said looking over the gear they had gathered together.

"How exactly are we going to do this without being too obvious? We need a smokescreen," said Fergus. "We need something that gives us a reason for hanging about on the pavement."

"Well, if we both take bikes then we can pretend we have a puncture. We can turn one bike upside down and be fixing it — supposedly. That should hide what we're doing on the pavement," said Murdo.

"That's probably about as good as we'll get," said Fergus. "There can't be many other reasons for spending time in one place on the pavement."

"Okay. Finally the biggest problem as I see it," he continued, "is how exactly do we get out at night when we're supposed to be tucked up in our beds?"

"That's easy!" said Murdo.

Ten minutes later Mrs. Fraser called Mrs. Speight. The two mothers found that that they had a good friend in common, so the conversation took forever to reach the subject of a sleepover in the caravan. However, when they finally heard Mrs. Fraser saying "Yes, Murdo does it all the time in the summer," they knew that the crucial moment had arrived.

"There we go, boys. That's fine," said Mrs. Fraser as she came off the phone. "Now, Murdo, the usual rules apply and I'll just explain them to Fergus so that he knows too. It's lights out when I say so, and lights out does not mean torches under the blankets. The door is locked by you and that's you in there for the night, okay?"

"Does it get any easier than that?" said Murdo back in the caravan. Fergus had to agree that the planning for the evening's expedition was going remarkably well, and things continued to go smoothly — at least, at first.

Fergus went back home for tea and to collect a few things for his night away, including his bike. The boys then spent the first part of the evening in the caravan getting Murdo's rucksack of equipment together. Jock dozed in his basket in the corner seemingly having had enough of the day's events. Murdo showed Fergus how the seats in the caravan could be turned into beds, and then the boys spent some time reading comics to distract themselves for an hour or two.

"Why have you got a computer in a hundred pieces?" Fergus asked, pointing to a pile of wires, memory cards and casing sticking out of a box in the corner behind Jock's basket.

Murdo looked unhappy. "There's supposed to be a function on the DataBoy that lets you transfer information from its memory to your PC. I was setting it up and thought that I would make some modifications to the hard drive but I hit a snag." Fergus thought that "snag" looked like a bit of an understatement for the random collection of parts.

"Have you got a computer?" asked Murdo.

"No ... I just use the one in the library sometimes but you can only get an hour at a time and there's always someone waiting to go on after you," said Fergus.

Eventually Mrs. Fraser popped her head round the door and suggested it was time for bed.

"Aw, Mum!" said Murdo putting on a bit of an act, since it would have seemed very odd if both boys revealed that they were delighted to have reached that stage of the evening. Switching off the lights as instructed, they then had the longest wait of the evening yet as the Frasers took the next hour to go to bed. Murdo twitched the curtain every few minutes to check if lights were still on in the house. Finally, after what seemed like an age, the last of the lights went off and after a few more minutes Murdo gauged that it was safe to go.

"Let's synchronize watches," he said putting on the

rucksack in the dark and pressing the light on his DataBoy. "I make it 23.14."

With these final preparations complete, the boys headed for the door. Jock sprang to his feet in anticipation. "No, Jock, you stay here," said Murdo in a firm whisper. Jock growled and barked twice. "No, Jock, not now," said Murdo looking despairingly at Fergus. "We might have to take him or he'll just start barking and Mum will know that something's up." Fergus nodded his agreement.

So Jock joined the boys as they slipped out of the Incident Room, pushed their bikes to the pavement and sped off. The Edinburgh summer night was clear and, with a full moon, it seemed more dark blue than black. In only a few minutes they were at the bottom of Comely Bank Avenue, had set their bikes up as planned and were crouched down as if involved in some essential bike maintenance. The road was quiet and with the plan starting so well, both boys were more excited than nervous. Even Jock seemed to have captured the mood, sniffing the air and pricking his ears up to be alert for any new sound.

In no time they were using the crowbar to begin lifting the manhole cover. Unfortunately, a few minutes later, they were still at the same stage. It was not budging an inch, and the afternoon spent with a pile of books and a casserole lid began to seem like a long and irrelevant time ago.

"Push harder," said Murdo. Fergus had by now turned brighter than the brightest red as he put every effort into leaning on the crowbar to try and prise the cover upwards.

"Can't ... do ... an-n-ny ... more," he squeezed out through gritted teeth. Murdo was hopping around behind him in agitation, giving what he obviously thought were helpful hints. Jock hopped around behind Murdo making what he obviously thought were encouraging panting noises.

"It'sssssss..s ... s-no good," said Fergus collapsing on to the pavement beside the manhole cover. Jock sniffed at the crowbar suspiciously and looked expectantly at Fergus, as did Murdo. Murdo might have been big, but he didn't consider himself to be strong and he looked very doubtful at the challenge offered by the manhole cover and the crowbar.

Fergus steeled himself for one last attempt and this time felt the manhole cover start to shift. "I think ... I think ..." he puffed between his teeth.

Jock panted ever more quickly and as Fergus said "I think ..." for the third time, the cover lifted a fraction. He yanked the crowbar to one side, just far enough to bring the cover down leaving a small opening.

Murdo set to work speedily, delving into his rucksack and pulling out the torch, but he soon found that the gap wasn't wide enough and the torch's beam wasn't strong enough, to enable them to see anything other than the first few feet of stone under the road surface. He switched to the next option of the walkman, microphone and string. Pressing the record button he fed the equipment through the gap they had created and lowered it down. "We'll let it run for a few minutes. If there's anything going on, we should be able to pick it up on this," he said tying the string round a rucksack strap and leaving the walkman dangling a few feet underground.

Feeling pleased that they would get something out of the evening's work after all, the boys were able to rest for a minute or two as the tiny tape recorder did its job. There were only a couple of cars passing by, and the drivers seemed oblivious to the boys on the pavement, huddled around upturned bikes. No one else seemed to be out and so the movement that Murdo saw out of the corner of his eye caught his attention immediately.

"Look over there," he whispered. "Is that a dog?"

Fergus looked over to the shadowy figure of an animal.

"It's a fox," said Fergus, "It comes round here quite a bit at night scavenging food from the rubbish."

Distracted from their task, the boys watched the fox

33

sniffing around at a bin bag that had been left on the pavement. Through the silence of the night they could hear the rattle of a can falling to the ground. Suddenly the silence was completely broken by furious barking. Jock, who had been patiently waiting as Fergus and Murdo had struggled with the manhole cover, had decided that the fox presented some form of danger to them all, and had taken matters into his own paws. By the time the boys realized what was happening, he was whizzing across the road on a collision course with the fox. Sensing that its evening meal was about to be interrupted the fox turned with a curious high-pitched bark, arched its back and stood snarling at Jock who was now speeding towards it like a canine missile. The fearless Jock stopped a few metres short of the fox, utterly convinced that he was saving the boys from some sort of terrible fate.

"Jock, be quiet," said Murdo sharply, but far too late considering that the night-time peace had been disrupted for almost half a minute already. Murdo grabbed his bike and crossed the road to try and break up the stand-off between Jock and the fox.

Sensing trouble as the noise showed no signs of stopping, Fergus quickly started gathering together the equipment when suddenly he was bathed in light. He whirled around to find an old lady peering through a brightly-lit window, which overlooked the pavement. He could see her scowling face clearly, although it seemed that she was having difficulty making out what was happening.

Jock's frenzied barking was making it clear that something out of the ordinary was taking place on Comely Bank Avenue. Breaking out into a panicky sweat, Fergus thought fleetingly that Murdo might let him off with this haphazard way of packing the rucksack given the pressure of being caught.

Murdo was still urging Jock to be quiet, but the little dog was barking as if his life and the lives of the boys depended on it. The fox was beginning to move away, but the fact that he was taking his time about it was making Jock even angrier and Murdo could do nothing to quieten his normally obedient dog.

Fergus strained to shove the manhole cover back into place. He knew that the only thing to do now was to get away from the scene as quickly as possible without a trace and without a noise.

"CLANG!" went the manhole cover as it dropped back into place. Fergus winced. He had added a fitting finale to the din of the last few minutes and had also closed the cover on the microphone lead chopping it in half, leaving him with the walkman and a cut wire and the rest lost below ground.

"What is going on? I'm going to call the police!" said a shrill voice behind him.

Fergus froze, sensing that the trouble was only just beginning. Looking around he saw that the old lady was now at her front door looking scared and angry at the same time.

"What do you think you're doing?" she said cautiously, beginning to come down her front path. Fergus looked around for support from Murdo and Jock but they were almost out of sight on the other side of the street. Jock's barking was finally subsiding as the fox had merged back into the shadows, and so Fergus was left looking like the source of the chaos.

"We ..." said Fergus feebly, beginning to explain and realizing that there wasn't a "we." There was only him.

"What were you doing at that manhole cover?" said the woman, before Fergus could go any further. "That's breaking and entering."

Fergus looked down, almost surprised to find a crowbar and a bulging rucksack at his feet.

"We were just trying to see if there was anything unusual underneath it," he said, choosing his words carefully, but realizing that this vague answer was unsatisfactory.

35

"We? Who is we?" said the old lady glaring at him. "The only unusual thing is that you appear to be trying to get inside a manhole cover outside my flat. Now that is unusual, would you not agree?"

There was a horrible silence as Fergus shuffled his feet and struggled to know what to say. Before he could stop himself he suddenly blurted out, "I stood on this cover and my watch went backwards and I want to know why!" As soon as he said it he knew it sounded ridiculous.

The woman's loud, angry voice changed to a scarier, steelier, quieter one. "I might be old but I'm not stupid," she said. "I recognize you, young man. I know where you live and I shall speak to your mother about this. Now kindly pick up all of your things and leave me in peace."

She stood with her arms folded and an expression that said that she had heard and said enough.

"I'm sorry to have bothered you," Fergus mumbled. Struggling to close the rucksack, he picked up his bike and began to head back up Comely Bank Avenue, feeling more embarrassed than he had ever done in his life.

As he trudged up the hill, Murdo emerged from the shadows looking slightly sheepish, knowing that Fergus had taken the brunt of the old woman's anger. Jock meanwhile trotted beside Murdo panting happily and looking up at the boys as if wanting to be congratulated on winning a famous victory.

"What did she say?" asked Murdo tentatively, but Fergus couldn't speak. Right now he didn't really care if his watch went forwards or backwards. He just wanted to go to bed, fall asleep and wake up thinking that this had all been a bad dream.

4. The Morning After the Night Before

What should have been a fun sleepover at the caravan became a long and sleepless night for Fergus. It wasn't the fact that he was in the unfamiliar surroundings of the caravan, it was the old lady's words ringing in his head that kept him awake. "I know where you live and I shall speak to your mother about this." He lay looking out at the full moon with his mind in turmoil. How much trouble could he get into, in one go? He decided that he would probably set a new record — being out at night without permission, trying to break into a manhole cover, disturbing the neighbours — he could hear it all now. He scrunched his eyes closed and squirmed in bed wishing he could turn the clock back. It seemed a bit ironic that the whole problem had arisen because his watch had gone backwards. Fergus was convinced without a shadow of a doubt that he would be grounded for months, and almost certainly banned from seeing Murdo again.

As if mirroring Fergus's mood, the next day was wet and gloomy. After breakfast in the Fraser's kitchen, the boys headed back to Comely Bank Avenue. Jock padded damply alongside.

"Did you have fun?" asked Mrs. Speight as the boys hung up their dripping jackets.

"Yeah it was great," said Fergus sounding as upbeat as he could. "We saw a fox," he added trying to inject some colour into the story. Jock licked his lips as if the word "fox" had reminded him of his dramatic encounter.

The boys made their excuses and spent the morning in Fergus's room looking through old annuals that Fergus had collected. Neither of them had the appetite to talk about cats and watches or anything remotely suggesting a mystery that needed to be solved. As the morning dragged on Murdo stood up, stretched and went to the window.

"Still wet," he said peering out through the rain-spattered pane at a car swishing by with its windscreen wipers flapping. Fergus joined him at the window, grimacing at the soggy summer scene.

"Looks like you've got a visitor," said Murdo nodding at a large flowery umbrella with a pair of legs sticking out from below. The figure stopped on the pavement before turning into number 81. Fergus peered more closely but couldn't see enough to make out who it was. Then just before it reached the door, the umbrella was pulled to one side and given a brisk shake which sent off a shower of droplets.

"Oh no," said Fergus turning pale. "We really are in trouble."

Murdo looked more closely and saw the old lady from the previous night. The boys looked at each other and both swallowed hard.

"Maybe she's just ... collecting for something?" Murdo said trying to be positive.

"Like for her collection of small boys' heads?" said Fergus, burying his head in his hands and groaning.

Before they could say any more, the doorbell rang. Fergus groaned again. Murdo moved to the bedroom door and opened it a crack to try and make out what was happening. He shrank back as Mrs. Speight came along the hall towards the front door. Fergus joined him, straining to hear what was said as the front door opened, but all that they could make out was a muffled exchange of voices. It was only as

Mrs. Speight headed back into the hall that they were able to hear properly.

"Well, you'd better come in then," was the first sentence that they both picked up clearly. At that, Fergus let out another groan. Murdo gave him a consoling pat on the shoulder.

The next moment, Mrs. Speight shouted, "Fergus, you've got a visitor." Her voice seemed to echo and hang in the hallway like the first of many accusations. Fergus looked at Murdo, and then at the window as he weighed up whether there was any means of escape.

"Fergus ...!" his mum called again more insistently. Knowing that there was nothing he could do but face the music, Fergus left his bedroom and trudged along the hall to the living room.

"I'll hang these up," Mrs Speight said as she came out of the living room carrying the woman's coat and umbrella. She raised a single questioning eyebrow as Fergus approached looking forlorn.

"Fergus," said his mum guiding him into the living room, "this is Mrs. Jenkins from down the road." Fergus edged slowly round the living room door. The old lady was sitting up straight in the armchair by the fire in a voluminous knitted cardigan. She looked Fergus straight in the eye and said, "Oh yes, Fergus and I have already met." Fergus began to go almost as pink as her cardigan.

Mrs. Speight looked a little confused by this exchange but politeness got the better of her and she didn't immediately enquire any further. Fergus knew, however, that it wouldn't be long before she found out just *how* he did know "Mrs. Jenkins from down the road."

"Right, well, I'll just put the kettle on," said Fergus's mum, giving Fergus a look that said, "I'll know everything shortly and I can already guess most of it."

"Tea with milk and two sugars would be just the ticket," said Mrs. Jenkins.

"Right you are," said Mrs. Speight with another piercing glance at Fergus as she left.

Fergus was finding it hard to look at Mrs. Jenkins. The last time he had seen her a few hours before, she was wagging her finger at him accusingly and now here she was sitting in the middle of his own front room. When he did summon up the courage to look at her, the adjustments she was making to the cushions behind her, along with some repeated throat clearing, suggested to Fergus that she was composing herself before making the big speech which would expose him as the neighbourhood's newest villain.

"So, Fergus," she said finally breaking the silence, "you must think that you are in a spot of bother."

"Aren't I?" said Fergus quietly, thinking that a "spot of bother" was an understatement for his situation.

"Frankly, when you gave me that ridiculous explanation last night about your watch, I told myself that not only did I have a troublemaker for a neighbour, but also one with a vivid imagination." Mrs. Jenkins adjusted herself to get more comfortable, and cleared her throat again as if she was about to say something that she was finding difficult.

"I now know," she continued, "that you were in fact telling the truth and I want to apologize."

There was a silence before Fergus could manage to blurt out just one word. "What ...?!"

"You appear to be correct," said Mrs. Jenkins, lowering her voice and looking at the door, as if not wanting anyone else to hear.

"Is your friend here at the moment?" she continued. "I presume the two of you are working together on this. Perhaps he should hear this too."

A minute later Fergus and Murdo were side by side on

the settee, still looking nervous but with the flickerings of relief on their faces.

Mrs. Speight appeared carrying a tray with tea, juice and biscuits. She couldn't contain her anxiety and curiosity any longer as she put it down on the coffee table.

"Is everything all right?" she said to Mrs. Jenkins. "You've got me rather worried. Have the boys done something wrong?"

"I assure you that everything is fine," said Mrs. Jenkins in a voice so kindly that the boys couldn't quite believe that it came from the same person who had interrupted their investigations the night before.

"Your son was a good neighbour yesterday and I'm really just here to say thank you."

Mrs. Speight looked baffled but slightly proud as she looked at Fergus and ruffled his hair. The boys both noticed that Mrs. Jenkins quickly winked at them out of the corner of her eye as Mrs. Speight was looking down at Fergus.

"Please don't let me hold you back, my dear, I'm sure you have lots to keep you busy. The boys and I can entertain each other," continued Mrs. Jenkins.

Fergus nearly choked on a biscuit as he saw his mother being asked to leave her own living room in such a gentle way that she seemed quite happy about it. Fergus's admiration for Mrs. Jenkins shot up even further. He had been practising for years and he could never have pulled off that trick. Here was a woman he needed to get to know.

"Oh well, I'll leave you to chat. Shout if you want a top-up," Mrs. Speight said, pointing at the teapot, and with that she left the room, closing the door behind her.

Mrs. Jenkins took a big slurp of her tea and a large chunk of biscuit, which she manoeuvred noisily around her mouth, clearly having a few problems with her teeth. The boys didn't quite know what to expect.

"I didn't sleep much last night," said Mrs. Jenkins breaking the silence again, putting her cup down and brushing her hands of biscuit crumbs. "All of that disturbance gave me a bit of a start I have to say. Anyway, this morning I went out with this." She rummaged in the baggy pocket of her pink cardigan and produced an old watch on a chain.

"This belonged to my husband, Stan, and it hasn't lost a minute in sixty years — until this morning when I stood on that manhole cover! What is going on down there?" She leaned towards the boys with a whisper.

"Well," said Murdo speaking for the first time and realizing that the elderly lady was rapidly becoming an unexpected ally, "we might have had a better idea what's going on if we hadn't been interrupted last night!"

They all laughed at this and any remaining tension in the room disappeared. For the next few minutes the boys showed Jessie their DataBoys and explained about their watches going into reverse. They went on to describe their side of the story from the previous night, including the fact that the abrupt end to the investigations which Jessie had caused, had resulted in the microphone wire being chopped in half.

"Oh, I am sorry about that. I must insist that you let me replace it as soon as possible," said Mrs. Jenkins. "I must say this is all very mysterious isn't it? It definitely sounds like something we need to get to the bottom of. Why don't you come down to my flat some time soon and we can get our heads together. I'll pass it with your mother of course, Fergus," she added.

"How about this afternoon?" said Murdo, his enthusiasm for mystery solving having reappeared dramatically in the last few minutes.

"Let me just see," said Mrs. Jenkins, fishing a small diary out of her cardigan pocket. Fergus wondered what else the bulging knitted pockets contained. She licked a finger and paged through the battered black book.

"No, I'm sorry, boys. I have my karate class at 2pm, and this evening I've got my Local History discussion group," she said matter-of-factly. "But this time tomorrow would be fine, if that suits you?"

The boys watched Mrs. Jenkins setting off down the front path. She looked pleased to see the rain had stopped and was jauntily swinging her umbrella as she headed away, limping slightly.

"Don't people usually learn karate when they're younger?" asked Murdo.

"And when they're able to jump around a bit?" added Fergus, wondering what other surprises were scheduled in Mrs. Jenkins' diary.

Fergus was relieved that Mrs. Jenkins had had a big chat with his mum before she left but not one that involved any details of the night before. In fact Mrs. Speight had tried to insist that Mrs. Jenkins stay for lunch but she had left saying that she never ate much before karate.

"She's great fun," said Fergus's mum. "I hope I'm like that when I'm that age."

"I suppose we'll find out in a couple of years," said Fergus ducking as his mum aimed a tea towel at his head.

Mrs. Jenkins' visit had left the boys in high spirits. As they made their way back to the Incident Room chatting about the value that some more help with the case might bring them, Murdo stopped in his tracks.

"The tape!" he shouted.

"What tape?" said Fergus.

"The tape from the walkman. We lost the microphone but we still have the tape and we haven't checked it yet!" said Murdo, breaking into a puffing run.

Back at the caravan Murdo rummaged around and in no time had rewound the tape and set it to play in a small cassette recorder. The first noises that the boys could hear were their own muffled voices, recorded when they had switched the walkman on and lowered it through the gap and into the manhole. These quickly disappeared and Murdo turned up the volume to maximum to see if the tape could offer more than just a humming sound.

"What's that?" said Fergus.

"What's what?" asked Murdo.

"That bleeping noise," said Fergus.

Both boys leaned into the cassette recorder to listen more carefully. Every so often there was a very distant single bleeping noise. Murdo got the stopwatch ready on his DataBoy and confirmed that thirty seconds passed between each bleep. Just before the tape cut off suddenly they heard more muffled noises but they were all from above ground with a hint of Jock's crazed barking.

"Well, I'm not sure what we really learned there," said Murdo.

"Other than the fact that something is bleeping under the pavement of Comely Bank Avenue," said Fergus. "Why don't we start thinking about the cats again. We seem to have hit a bit of a dead end with the watches for now."

With that, the boys started looking through Murdo's notes on the interviews that he had completed with all of the cat owners, to see if there were any common links between the disappearances. It seemed that most owners reported that their cats had been behaving normally in the time leading up to their disappearance. They had gone on to describe themselves as being baffled as to what might have happened to their cat, and that they thought it was very out of character for their pets to disappear in this fashion. The boys had read five or six sets of interview notes when Fergus spotted an emerging theme. "Don't all of these people say that the first time they noticed their cat was missing was early in the morning?"

Murdo flicked back over the notes and nodded in agreement. Fergus continued with his line of reasoning, "So maybe it's just the owners who allow their cats out at night whose pets go missing. What if something is happening at night to these cats?"

The boys worked hard during the afternoon looking through every set of interview notes just to establish at what time each cat had gone missing. Sure enough, the pattern that Fergus had spotted proved to be true for every single cat.

"This is a major breakthrough," concluded Murdo pacing around as much as he could within the confines of the caravan. "A significant development," he added.

"But what does it mean?" said Fergus.

Murdo stopped in his tracks. "I have absolutely no idea."

Despite this, the boys finished the day feeling positive that they had begun to make some sense out of all the information that Murdo had gathered, even if they didn't quite know where it might lead.

The following day Murdo arrived on his scooter with Jock tagging along behind and the boys walked down Comely Bank Avenue to Mrs. Jenkins' flat.

"Come in, come in," she said to the boys. Jessie bustled her way through the dimly lit hall of her ground floor flat. "Right, you boys go through to the living room there," she said pointing to a room on the right. She headed off along the hall chatting cheerily to herself about "getting a tray organized," her baggy cardigan almost knocking a vase of flowers off a rickety hall table as she went.

Fergus led the way cautiously into the living room. As he pushed the door open, it felt like going back in time. Their first impressions were that the room was dingy and dull, but as their eyes adjusted to the gloom they could see that there was plenty of interest.

The floral-patterned wallpaper was difficult to see because there were so many framed black and white photographs, and paintings of landscapes and farms. A big clock with a long pendulum and weights hanging on dark brassy chains was attached to the wall near the fireplace.

"Look at that," said Murdo pointing to a large framed photo on top of the mantlepiece. A white cat looked back at them.

"Look at this," Fergus said with wonder in his voice, pointing to one corner of the room where there was a very new, very shiny, and very, very large computer on a table. "This lady is full of surprises," said Fergus shaking his head slowly. Murdo went over to the computer and peered at the books lying beside it. "*You're Never Too Old to Learn, Crash Course in Computers, Grannies Can Surf Too*," he read out.

Before the boys could find any more surprises, Mrs. Jenkins appeared behind them. "Here we are," she said, carrying a tray into the room and setting it down on a dusty coffee table.

"Ah, you've found my latest purchase," she said seeing the boys standing beside her computer. "It's top of the range!"

The boys looked stunned. "Don't look so surprised," said Mrs. Jenkins, "I might be ancient but I do live in the 21st century you know," she said with a sly smile. "Now, how about this?" she said turning her attention to the tray. "Not only am I a computer geek but I also bake the best cakes in Edinburgh."

Jock had already worked this out and was sniffing impatiently at the edge of the coffee table. Neither he nor the boys needed a second invitation to tuck in to the plate of rock buns, pancakes and shortbread. They munched away happily, grinning to each other as Mrs. Jenkins chatted and asked them questions about the backwards watches. However, there really wasn't much more that the boys could tell her, and so the conversation soon went quiet.

Murdo asked innocently, "Is that your cat, Mrs. Jenkins?" nodding towards the photo on the mantlepiece.

"Now, boys," said Mrs. Jenkins seriously, "If we are to become friends, and I hope we shall, you will have to get one thing straight." Murdo looked embarrassed, thinking that he was being too personal with his line of questioning. However, Mrs. Jenkins wasn't bothered by Murdo's question.

"It's Jessie. You must call me Jessie. I'm afraid I won't be able to provide any more homebaking if you call me Mrs. Jenkins. That sort of name would be some strange old dear who lived on her own and who everyone avoided. Jessie on the other hand, is the name of someone who regularly produces pancakes for private investigators." The boys smiled and Murdo looked especially pleased at this description.

"Now that we've cleared up that little issue Murdo, yes, that it is my cat, Jasper, but I'm afraid that the poor old thing has gone missing. I haven't seen him for a fortnight."

The boys glanced at each other and stopped chewing at the same time.

"What is it?" said Jessie suddenly distracted from her teacup by the boys' reaction.

"Well," said Fergus cautiously looking at Murdo for approval, "we're actually trying to solve two mysteries. Murdo can explain better since he's been on the case for longer than me." Picking up the story, Murdo took the next few minutes to tell Jessie all that he knew about the forty-three missing cats, the Incident Room and the interviews that he had carried out with cat owners in the area.

Jessie listened intently, occasionally asking questions and nodding, but when Murdo had finished she just sat shaking her head slowly. The boys sat in silence. "Don't you believe him?" asked Fergus eventually.

"Oh yes," said Jessie looking up brightly, "I'm just shaking my head to make sure all of the information sinks in evenly. That is quite a story, boys. So my Jasper isn't the only one. I suppose that's reassuring in a way."

Jessie stood up and began walking round the room, her pink cardigan flapping as she shook the stiffness first out of one leg and then the other. "Well, you've got two big mysteries on your hands here, haven't you? This calls for quite an investigation, quite an investigation."

The boys smiled and nodded.

"Jessie, what time of day did Jasper disappear?" said Fergus, suddenly remembering the significant discovery of the previous day.

Jessie thought for a minute. "Let me see now. It was a Wednesday and we had our breakfast together. He often went out after that, but he was around again at teatime when I came in from karate. He went out again during the evening. I looked to see if he wanted to come in for the night, but he wasn't around. That wasn't unusual so I just locked up. When I opened the front door at breakfast time I would have expected to see him sitting on the doorstep, but there was no sign of him. I haven't seen him since." Jessie sighed and dabbed at her eyes, "You probably think that I'm just a daft old dear for getting upset but I did talk away to Jasper any time he was in the flat. He has been a very faithful friend ever since my husband, Stan, died. I particularly miss him at breakfast. We would sit down together and eat peanut butter and marmite on toast every day. The start of the day just isn't the same any more."

Both Murdo and Fergus decided that it wasn't the time to comment on the bizarre choice of food that Jasper ate.

"I can't imagine losing Jock," said Murdo. "It must be awful."

Fergus told Jessie of the recurring pattern of nighttime disappearances. Their new friend seemed reassured once again that she was by no means the only one faced with this predicament.

"I suppose you've got a database that helped you spot these patterns?" asked Jessie. The boys looked blankly at her. "Now don't tell me you two aren't computerized?" she quizzed them further, putting down her teacup in consternation.

"Neither of us have computers right now," said Murdo. "But I do have a very good filing system," he added defensively. Fergus nodded supportively beside him, but suspected that this was a line of questioning that Jessie was not about to let go.

"Boys, I don't want to appear like I'm telling you how to run the show, but I do think that there's a lot you could be missing out on by not using a computer for your investigations. Now you are very welcome to use mine if you like and I can always help. I've reached Level 7 in *Databases for Old Dears*, you know," she said winking at them.

Murdo grinned at Fergus. They both knew that they had not only acquired a new ally in their investigations but a serious piece of computer hardware into the bargain.

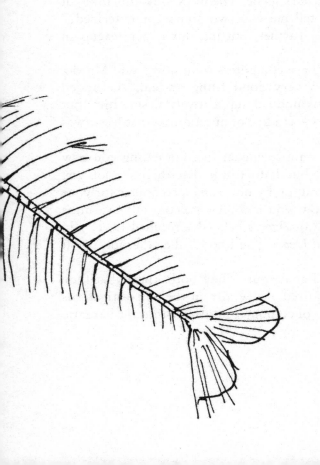

5. The Bait

Jessie and the boys spent the next couple of hours huddled around the computer, by the end of which they had achieved a number of things, or "followed up a number of lines of enquiry," as Murdo preferred to describe it.

Firstly, Jessie reminded them that they had all met because of backwards watches and not missing cats, so they trooped out to the manhole cover and watched each of their watches go backwards. Back inside Jessie checked the internet for the company that manufactured DataBoys and sent a quick email off to Customer Services to enquire if they had ever had complaints about the watches going backwards before. She also clicked onto the "Frequently Asked Questions" page of the company website to check that there wasn't a standard response to the slightly odd question, "Why does my watch go backwards when I stand on the manhole cover at the bottom of Comely Bank Avenue?" Perhaps, unsurprisingly, the three investigators found that this didn't feature alongside questions about how to use some of the Twenty Funky Functions and how to buy replacement straps, which Murdo was delighted to see.

Next, Jessie suggested that they switch their attention to the cats. "Multi-tasking! Fantastic!" declared Murdo, delighted that they were now tackling both mysteries at the same time. The first step was an internet search using the words "lost," "cats" and "Edinburgh." This revealed everything from information about the Edinburgh Cat and Dog Home for lost pets, a couple of websites set up by owners of lost cats that Murdo recognized from his interviews, and even research into the eating habits of cats by an Edinburgh University student.

Although the boys didn't feel they had come up with any more answers, it felt good to be covering a few new angles.

Finally, and in no time at all, Jessie set up a simple database where each missing cat's name, description, contact details and the date, time and location of their disappearance could all be entered. The boys started by keying in Jasper's details, followed by another dozen or so cats from Murdo's file, and they promised to come back and complete the database over the next couple of days.

"I'm sure this will unlock some secrets for us," said Jessie, patting the computer.

As Jessie waved the boys goodbye from her front door she called out, "I think that we'll make a very good team working together." Murdo looked pleased enough to pop.

Fergus returned home happy with the work of the previous few hours. As he unlocked the front door he could hear his mum chatting to someone.

"Fergus, can you come here for a minute," she called from the living room.

As he walked into the room, Fergus nearly tripped over a large shiny, Siamese cat sitting on the floor. His mind immediately whirred into action as he wondered how one of the missing cats had magically appeared in the middle of the front room.

"It's all right, she doesn't bite," said a smiling young woman with short hair and casual clothes.

Mrs. Speight spoke up. "Fergus, this is Narveen. You've probably seen her before. She lives at number 89. She's going away for a long weekend and wants us to look in on Sasha while she's away," she said nodding towards the cat by the door. "I said that you and I could help. What do you think?"

Before Fergus had a chance to answer, Narveen chipped in, as if concerned that Fergus might be about to say no. "You just have to put out half a tin of food a couple of times a day and give her a wee bit of chat. She's pretty independent really and she'll spend a lot of time out and about."

Fergus looked at the cat and broke into a huge smile. "Brilliant!" he said, his mind switching from the idea that this was a lost cat to the possibility of using it to find some of its missing friends. Then, as if remembering where he was, he added, "Eh yeah, we'd love to look after her."

"There you go," said Mrs. Speight to Narveen. "An enthusiastic new recruit!"

Narveen started to reply and although Fergus knew she was talking to him, he couldn't help his mind racing off in another direction. He and Murdo had just been handed a cat on a plate. Cat bait! They could track this cat and see if it led them to the lost cats. It was perfect.

"Fergus?" said his mum, getting slightly irritated that her son had switched off when a visitor was talking to him.

"What ... er ... yeah ... great, yeah ... love to, great," he said.

"Thanks, Fergus," said Narveen. "Do you like animals?"

"Yeah, my friend Murdo has a dog called Jock and he's really cool. Murdo's really interested in cats as well though. Would he be able to help us with Sasha?" said Fergus to both Narveen and his mum.

"Fergus and Murdo are thick as thieves at the moment," Mrs. Speight said by way of explanation to Narveen, "I'm not sure what they're up to half the time, but they seem happy."

"Well, Sasha won't know what's happening if she starts to get lots of attention," said Narveen. "I tend to leave her to her own devices, but I'm sure she'll enjoy the change."

Fergus looked at Sasha. She looked back at Fergus. Fergus could have sworn that the cat could tell what he was thinking and was saying through narrowed eyes, "Don't bother me with your silly games, little boy."

"I'll be away from Thursday," said Narveen bringing out a set of keys from her handbag. "I'll leave tins of food in the kitchen, along with her bowl. There'll be a note with my number and the emergency vet's number, but I can't imagine any reason why you'd need them. You'll be fine, won't you, snookums?" she said picking up the rather bored looking Siamese and nuzzling it.

Fergus might have felt enthusiastic about looking after the cat, but he couldn't quite imagine himself getting that affectionate with it over the next few days. He would certainly be drawing the line at calling it "snookums." Fergus concluded quietly that he would be quite happy if Sasha was always at arm's length but led him to the location of another forty-three cats; forty-four now that they knew Jasper was missing too.

"Mum, can I go round to Murdo's?" said Fergus suddenly desperate to do the next bit of planning at the Incident Room. Mrs. Speight gave a smile towards Narveen as if to say, "See what I mean?" and said, "Well okay, as long as you're back for tea." Narveen thanked Fergus again for helping out, before he sped off on his bike to launch another new line of enquiry.

Minutes later in the Incident Room, Murdo was pacing up and down. "What a gift! What an opportunity!" he said. "We have bait for seventy-two hours. If all goes well, this could crack the case. Imagine if this cat goes where the missing cats are and we're right there on its tail!"

"Sasha won't like that!" joked Fergus, forgetting that there was a time and a place for humour with Murdo, who was now glaring at him for bursting his bubble of enthusiasm.

Murdo shook his head briskly as if to get rid of the interruption. "So this neighbour of yours goes away on Thursday afternoon and the first feed is on Friday morning. We need to pack provisions for a day's cat-tracking. Let's start a list of what we need."

Murdo began a typically frenetic session of equipment-gathering, but came across a hitch when he decided that one essential item was a street plan of the city.

"Mum, have you seen my city map?" he asked after they had exhausted their search of the Incident Room and most of the house.

"I think I might have seen it in Heather's room," said Mrs. Fraser. "She had it for some school project."

Murdo paled and looked for a moment like he might reconsider just how essential this item actually was to the next stage of their investigations. However, after a deep breath he seemed to gather himself together. "We mustn't let this jeopardize our research," he said as they headed somewhat tentatively upstairs, with Jock following close behind.

Fergus wasn't expecting to see a flowery nameplate on Heather's bedroom door and he wasn't disappointed. The door sported a "No Entry" sign in the middle alongside official notices saying that not only were radioactive materials and corrosive products stored in the room, but also that safety helmets should be worn at all times. This helpful advice was capped off nicely by a large skull and crossbones. If the door wasn't off-putting enough, the screaming guitars and anguished vocals of the music blaring through it suggested that Heather did not want to be interrupted.

Murdo took a deep breath and knocked firmly on the door. Silence. The music cut out as if the door was linked to the sound system.

He knocked again. Silence.

Taking this as a cue for his next move, Murdo put his hand slowly towards the door handle as if it might electrocute him. Holding his breath he opened the door and entered the room. Jock stuck close to Murdo's leg sensing that his master needed all the allies he could get. He began growling as menacingly as a small dog could.

Heather was sitting cross-legged on her bed surrounded by magazines, with the wall behind her covered in posters of grungy-looking bands. She didn't look up as the door opened. "Did I say you could come in?"

"You didn't actually say anything," said Murdo trying to sound confident.

Heather looked at him. Fergus decided that this was probably quite a good start. She could have ignored him completely after all.

"I need my street map back," said Murdo.

"Your street map," said Heather.

"Yes," said Murdo.

"Now why exactly would I want to give that to you?" asked Heather.

"Mainly because it's mine," said Murdo.

"What about you, Fergus, do you think I should give it to him?" said Heather turning her attention to Fergus.

"Er ... well obviously it's up to you, but we do need it," said Fergus.

"Oh, so polite," said Heather sweetly. "What do you need to use it for, Dr. Watson? Still helping Sherlock with the big case?"

Murdo fired a warning glance at Fergus.

"We only need it for the day," said Fergus, feeling pleased that he had managed to deflect the question.

At this point a phone rang and Heather made a dive for a mobile buried beneath the magazines on her bed. "Hi ... yeah ..., nothing much, what about you?" she said to someone who was obviously far more interesting to her than the boys. Spotting his opportunity Murdo moved quickly and grabbed the street map, which he had seen sticking out of a pile of schoolbooks. Seconds later, the boys were charging down the stairs feeling like they had pulled off a successful mission into enemy territory.

"Saved by the bell!" laughed Murdo jumping the last three stairs and making the house rock as he landed.

"She is seriously scary," said Fergus hot on his heels. "Has she always been like that?"

"Mum says it's a teenage thing. Do you think we'll get like that too?" said Murdo with genuine concern in his voice.

On Friday morning, Fergus was just going into Narveen's flat with his mum when Murdo appeared in typical fashion, zooming down the hill on his scooter, his rucksack bursting at the seams. For once there was no sign of Jock as Murdo had decided wisely that following a cat from a distance might be too much of a challenge for him.

Mrs. Speight felt forced to comment on Murdo's habit of carting so much equipment around with him as she unlocked Narveen's front door, "I'm surprised you don't topple over with that weight on. Are you sure you have enough things with you?" she said jokingly.

As serious as ever, Murdo replied, "Well I do hope so. I've planned for a full day's work." Fergus smiled at his mum. She in turn raised an eyebrow and smiled. They both liked Fergus's new and slightly eccentric friend.

"So what are you two going to do today?" asked Mrs. Speight as she emptied half a tin of cat food into Sasha's bowl.

"Murdo is doing a project on cat behaviour," said Fergus quickly. "We're going to spend the day tracking Sasha — you know, see where she goes and what she gets up to."

"Well, good luck, but she could well be faster than you ... especially if you're carrying all that extra baggage with you," Mrs. Speight said smiling at Murdo.

"So what *have* you got in there?" asked Fergus later, pointing to the rucksack as the boys sat on the doorstep. The start of their exciting day's tracking had proved not to be very exciting at all as Sasha was sitting on the front step of number 89 soaking up the sun, with no apparent intention of going anywhere.

"Binoculars, file of missing cats, filofax, money, notebook, packed lunch, pencils, pens, street plan, toolkit, torch." said Murdo in one breath and in worryingly accurate alphabetical order.

Fergus nodded slowly. "You missed the kitchen sink," he said.

"Better over-prepared than under-prepared, Fergus," said Murdo in a superior voice. There were times when Fergus was with Murdo that he wanted to glance at someone and roll his eyes, but unfortunately someone wasn't always available. He looked over at Sasha instead.

"She's off!" he shouted, realizing that the cat had suddenly picked herself up from her slumbering position on the front step and was heading off down Comely Bank Avenue.

In one move, Murdo threw on his rucksack and had the time of this first development noted neatly down in his notebook. The tracking had begun and the boys headed off at a fast pace to keep up with the Siamese, who was padding purposefully away from the flat.

Almost immediately the boys were faced with their first problem. They had not bargained on the fact that Sasha had no respect for property or privacy. It wasn't long before she was sniffing in gardens and the boys found themselves hanging around outside people's houses for longer than they felt was really acceptable. The memory of being challenged by Jessie was still fresh in their minds, even though that encounter had turned out for the best.

At the bottom of Comely Bank Avenue they found themselves loitering close to Jessie's flat as Sasha nosed around in a nearby front garden, and the boys agreed it would be good to keep her informed of their latest approach to solving the mystery. Fergus ran over and rang her bell, anxiously looking back to check that he wasn't missing a sudden change in direction by Sasha.

"Ah, Fergus! What a lovely surprise."

Fergus turned back to find Jessie at the door with a drill in her hand and a pencil tucked behind her ear. Despite wearing overalls Fergus noticed that she still had her pink cardigan on. He didn't have to say anything as the expression on his face clearly asked, "What on earth are you doing?!"

"Just putting up a shelf," she said by way of explanation.

"Well, I'm just letting you know that we're tracking a neighbour's cat to see if that gives us any new leads," said Fergus.

"Good thinking. Keep me posted and give me a call if there's anything I can help with," Jessie said cheerily.

"Quick, Fergus," shouted Murdo in the distance. "She's getting away!"

The Siamese had suddenly picked up speed and seconds later she shot across the road, dodging a moped and two cars, and completely ignoring the red man on the pedestrian crossing. The boys came to an abrupt halt at the edge of the pavement, weighing up the traffic rather more carefully than Sasha had done, and deciding that the cat was more of a risk-taker than they were. They craned their necks around the passing cars to try to see her. She seemed to have slowed to a saunter again on the far side of road as if she were toying with the boys.

"I've heard of playing cat and mouse but this is ridiculous," said Fergus, as they finally got a green man to cross the road and were able to continue their pursuit of the mischievous cat who was now heading for the nearby park.

"It should be nice and easy to keep a track of her here," said Murdo confidently, "Lots of open spaces." As if to deliberately prove him wrong, Sasha leapt up on a high wall running along one side of the park, walked along a section of it, looked back at the boys and then jumped down the other side disappearing completely from view. Fergus closed his eyes slowly and shook his head in disbelief. The day looked like being over before it had even begun.

"This will *not* stop us!" said Murdo with a sudden shout of determination. "Quick, Fergus, let me get up on your shoulders! We need to see where she's gone."

"Er ... no disrespect, but wouldn't it be easier the other way around?" asked Fergus, weighing up the options and deciding that he did not want to be underneath Murdo.

Murdo mumbled a bit and squatted down saying, "Come on then! Hurry up! There's no time to waste, she could be getting away!"

Fergus climbed gingerly on to Murdo's shoulders and began to straighten up, feeling his way up the wall as Murdo puffed and panted and tried to stand up. Fergus eventually managed to get his hands onto the top, although this was more to do with how light he was rather than how strong Murdo was. It was a very high wall and in order to see over it, Fergus had to haul himself up the last few inches, finishing with his elbows on top of the wall and his feet dangling just above Murdo's shoulders. He peered into a well-kept garden.

"Oi, what are you doing?" said a man emerging from a greenhouse. "Right, this is the last time. Marjory, call the police!"

"Wh ... What?!" said Fergus.

"Every week, kids like you come climbing over our walls and chucking stones at my greenhouse. The police told us just to call them, so that's exactly what I'm going to do ... Marjory!" He was bawling in the direction of the house and Fergus could see movement behind one of the windows.

"But I was just, just ..." started Fergus.

"There is *no* reason for doing whatever you are doing," said the man striding towards Fergus and a nearby gate in the wall.

"Murdo, get me down from here," Fergus shouted, trying to connect his dangling feet with Murdo's shoulders. He was having trouble making contact and bent his head down so that he could see what he was doing. One glance explained everything. Not only were Murdo's shoulders not there — none of Murdo was. Fergus felt anger and embarrassment flash across his face knowing that he had been stranded.

"Right you. Get down from there!" The man's voice was behind him now. He hadn't wasted any time in reaching Fergus, who guessed that "Marjory" was already on the phone to the nearby police station.

"Come on, get down!" said the man.

"Er, I can't," said Fergus waggling his legs to show that they were a long way off the ground. The man grabbed his legs roughly and "helped" him down from the wall.

"How did you get up there?" snapped the man.

"My friend ..." Fergus's sentence tailed off.

"Scarpered has he?" said the man, "Well at least I've got one of you. Right ... name." The man had whipped out a notebook from his back pocket, and Fergus couldn't stop himself thinking that this could be a glimpse of what Murdo would be like in forty years time — notebook and pen at the ready.

"Fergus Speight," said Fergus mournfully.

"So, what do you think you were doing trying to get into my garden?" demanded the man.

"Well, I wasn't really, I was just trying to see where a cat had gone," replied Fergus.

"Oh, I see," said the man his voice loaded with sarcasm. "You were just taking it for a walk were you?"

"Something like that," said Fergus weakly.

For the next few minutes Fergus was faced with a barrage of questions about where he lived, who he lived with and just what exactly he had been up to on top of the garden wall. Throughout the interrogation the man licked the tip of his pencil before officiously writing each answer in his notebook. Fergus was just beginning to get used to the idea that he had been caught in the act, when he glimpsed a police car pulling up and a policewoman and a policeman getting out. He felt his legs go wobbly.

"Ah, good," said the man snapping shut his notebook.

"Officer, my name is Marshall and it was my wife that called the station. I have apprehended the culprit," he bellowed at the approaching police.

"Hallo there," said the policewoman as she reached them. "What have you been up to then?" she said directly to Fergus.

"I was trying to find a cat. It had jumped up on the wall and then disappeared."

"A likely story! Officer, I ask you!" said Mr. Marshall, addressing the policeman and ignoring the policewoman.

"Yes sir, if you'll just let me talk to the boy for a minute," said the policewoman. "Right then ... my name is Gill Hall. I'm the Community Police Officer. What's your name?"

PC Gill Hall patiently asked Fergus where he lived, what he had been doing and how exactly he had got up on to the wall. When she asked "Where's your friend now?" Fergus was tempted to shout, "I don't know and he's not really my friend any more!"

Fergus found that he was having difficulty explaining why he was following a cat. He thought that it might test the officer's patience to start talking about the mysterious disappearance of forty-four cats. Suddenly there was a shout behind him. "Fergus, there you are. Have you had any luck? Have you found him?"

It was Jessie looking rather flushed from running in overalls and a cardigan. Beside her was a red-faced Murdo, equally unused to running. "I brought the cavalry!" he said.

"Officer, if there's a problem here it's my fault," said Jessie. "I asked the boys to look for my cat, Jasper, and they were enthusiastically doing exactly what I asked them. Please accept my apologies."

"What kind of cat was it?" said Mr. Marshall suspiciously.

"A Siamese," said Murdo as quickly as he could, knowing that Jessie might start to describe Jasper.

"I didn't ask you!" snapped Mr. Marshall.

"I appreciate that you are upset," said Jessie. "However, there is no need to be so impolite."

"I think we have a bit of a misunderstanding here," said Gill Hall. "Boys, I would recommend that if you are following a cat and it goes into someone's garden that you ring their bell to ask permission to go any further. No more climbing on walls. This is private property after all."

"You mean that's it!" said Mr. Marshall, his face turning from bright red to a deep maroon. "Aren't you going to charge him or, or take him away?"

"Mr. Marshall, I appreciate your concern. However on this occasion it's just some over-enthusiasm and the boys were trying to do a genuine good deed."

Mr. Marshall made a rather peculiar strangled noise and began to go purple. Fergus was sure he would have preferred to see him and Murdo behind bars for their behaviour and the way he was looking at Jessie suggested that he would be happy to see her join them. Gill Hall brought the incident to a close in a diplomatic way, leaving everyone with a note of her telephone number should they ever need it. She was both amused and impressed as Murdo

63

immediately entered it into the memory function of his DataBoy.

"Thanks, Jessie, you were brilliant," said Fergus a few minutes later as they headed back to Comely Bank Avenue.

"Not at all, boys. But you will have to be more careful," said Jessie. "We need to work out a more trouble-free way of proceeding with the case."

"YOO HOO! Fergus! YOO HOO! Jessica!" Fergus and Jessie both winced at the sudden piercing cry behind them. "Do you know Beryl Scrimgeour too?" asked Fergus. Jessie nodded looking slightly weary as she turned and mustered a smile at the approaching vision in blue.

"Go now," hissed Fergus to Murdo. "Save yourself before it's too late! I'll call you!" Murdo looked slightly confused but didn't stay around for an explanation and he began to jog away in as athletic a manner as his bulky frame allowed.

"HALLO FERGUS, JESSICA, how are you both? Ah Jessica, I see you have been busy as usual," she said acknowledging Jessie's overalls. "I must say that the job you did hanging my mirror has been absolutely first rate. Jessica, you must come round soon so that I can thank you properly. We could spend the afternoon catching up. It's been a while since we had a good chat."

Fergus noted that Jessie seemed to gather herself together before giving her biggest smile. "That would be lovely, Beryl. I will call you soon. Now I am going to be very rude because I know that Fergus's mother is expecting him home and I don't want her to get concerned." Fergus nodded seriously beside her. "Meanwhile I have to change because I'm due elsewhere in twenty minutes, so do forgive us both for rushing off."

Much to Fergus's amazement Mrs. Scrimgeour miraculously began to back off. "Oh absolutely, of course, but do pop in soon, Jessica — I really must repay you in some way. FERGUS, DO SEND MY GREETINGS TO YOUR MOTHER!" she bawled after them as Jessie and Fergus walked away with a final wave at the disappearing figure in blue.

"It's rather unkind of me but I have thought about nailing her lips together," said Jessie when they were just out of earshot. Fergus smiled, still marvelling at Jessie's skills in completing the shortest conversation that he had ever been involved in with Beryl Scrimgeour.

Although it was only mid-morning Fergus had just about had enough of their investigations for the day. Sasha was long gone and with her any possibility of carrying on their day's tracking. The much-planned expedition had achieved absolutely nothing.

"How did you get on?" asked Mrs. Speight as Fergus arrived back at number 81.

"She lost us pretty quickly. I think she's done that sort of thing before," said Fergus.

"Well cats are quite independent, aren't they? They're pretty definite about what they like and don't like."

"Mmm, I suppose so," said Fergus wondering at the same time if his mother's observation might have some link with the disappearance of forty-four cats.

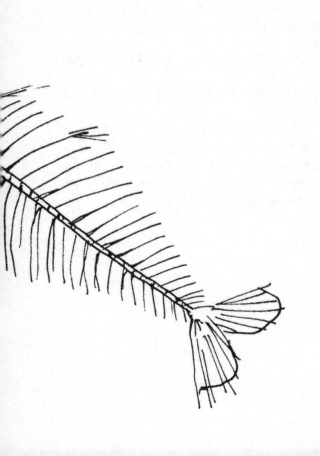

6. The Vaults

Early the next morning Fergus's mum found that Sasha was back next door as usual, having used the catflap to get back into the flat. "She said that she was being followed by a couple of boys yesterday but managed to shake them off," said Mrs. Speight. "Ha ha, very funny," said Fergus quietly pleased that Sasha was safe and sound.

When the phone went just after breakfast time and Fergus's mum spent the first few minutes in cheerful conversation, Fergus realized that it was Jessie she was speaking to. When she finally passed it to him, Jessie's instructions were quite clear. "I'd like you and Murdo to come down this morning. I've got my hands on something that I think you might find interesting."

Jessie had left an air of mystery about what exactly she had "got her hands on," so as the boys headed down the hill in the mid-morning sun with Jock padding alongside, they speculated on what it might be. Murdo suggested that she might have bought a new piece of software for her computer before they had even had a chance to get the hang of the old stuff. Fergus speculated that she might want to show them a new karate move or that, knowing Jessie, there was even an outside chance that she had dug a tunnel from the middle of her living room into the manhole outside. Whatever it was, the boys agreed that with Jessie anything was possible.

Minutes later they were being led along the hall in Jessie's flat. "Sit down boys," she said pointing to the chairs at the kitchen table in a no-nonsense manner. The table was bare except for a long cardboard tube. The boys now knew Jessie well enough to tell that she meant business this morning. She hadn't even put the kettle on, let alone given them a sniff of her home baking. As they dutifully took their seats, Jessie began to take two long rolls of paper out of the cardboard tube. "These are most revealing, most revealing," said Jessie as she did so. She unrolled the large pieces of paper on the table in front of them and pinned down the corners with jars of jam, honey and pickle from the worktop behind her. "There!" she said grandly as she placed the last jar triumphantly and stood back. "What do you make of that?"

Murdo and Fergus leaned in closer and looked at the large plan in front of them. They then quickly glanced at each other in ways that said, "What is it?" and "I don't know, you tell me!"

Even Jock looked quizzically from Murdo to Fergus and whined.

Fergus looked up at Jessie with what he hoped was an encouraging smile and then looked at the plan, sensing that Jessie was waiting for them both to agree that the paper covered in lines and symbols was in fact "most revealing."

"I'm sorry, Jessie," said Murdo finally, "But what are we looking at?"

Jessie looked a bit taken aback, looked at the plans and looked at the boys.

"It's where we want to see! No more lifting manhole covers in the dark!" she said.

The boys looked at her blankly.

"Underground," she said, "We can see underground!"

Jessie went on to explain what the plans showed. The first one with boxes and straight lines was an overhead view of all of the numbered properties on Raeburn Place and the streets nearby up to Comely Bank Avenue. The second plan, which Jessie concentrated on more, showed a side view of the buildings on Raeburn Place but more interestingly went on down the page to show what was below street level. As the boys absorbed the detail of arches and lines drawn on the plan, both realized that they were looking at passageways and cellars underneath the shops and beyond, reaching almost as far as Jessie's flat. As Jessie enthused about the plans, Fergus spotted the small title box in one corner of the plan that stated in neat script "Raeburn Place Vaults 1927" and nudged Murdo to show him.

"Where did you get these, Jessie?" asked Murdo.

"My husband, Stan, used to work at the Council. One of his colleagues is still there, and has kept in touch with me since Stan died. He's in the Planning Department now and I asked him how you would go about finding out what a particular manhole was covering. He just asked me which manhole cover and came up with this."

"So which shops are above each of these cellars then? And which are closest to our manhole cover?" asked Fergus as he continued to stare at the plans.

Jessie pulled up a chair. "I walk past them everyday but I couldn't be certain which ones are exactly where, especially since some of them come and go in such a short space of time. I was thinking that you two could nip out and make a list of the current shops at this end of Raeburn Place and then we can add them into the plan." Jessie reached for two notebooks and pens from beside her phone. "What do you think?"

Fergus and Murdo readily agreed and decided to split the task by each taking one side of the street. When Jessie announced that she could bake rock buns in the half an hour that it would take the boys to get their lists, Murdo disappeared in a flash, Jock scampering at his heels and for once Fergus almost managed to keep up with him.

Sure enough, they arrived back breathlessly at the front doorstep thirty minutes later to be met by Jessie, complete with her oven gloves and a dusting of flour on her cardigan declaring that the rock buns were ready. Back at the kitchen table, the boys started reading through their list of shops in between mouthfuls of hot home baking.

"The Copper Kettle Café, Crockett's Watches and Clocks, Stein's the Fishmonger, Geraldine's Gift Shop, Curlz Hairdressers," read Fergus. "Wright's Travel Agent, Double-Quick Dry Cleaners, Pete's Pizzas," read Murdo as Jessie wrote the names on to the boxes that depicted the shops.

In ten minutes the Raeburn Place shops were all named and the plan now showed that the shop, whose cellar seemed to be underneath the manhole cover, was called Capital Computing.

"That's where I bought my computer. It's quite a new place," said Jessie. "They were a very nice bunch of lads, I must say."

"So why would standing on a manhole cover above the cellar of a computer shop make your watch go backwards?" asked Fergus bracing himself as he noticed Murdo's eyes widening.

"Well ..." began Murdo, "maybe they have some *massive* computer down there giving off some *huge* electrical charge that gives off *billions* of positive and negative electrons and stuff like that is buzzing around and sucking time into some spiralling vortex, which is spinning underground but creates this subterranean force that transmits through the ground to affect any clock or watch within a two mile radius and ..."

"Have you quite finished, Murdo?" said Jessie with a smile, trying to interrupt him in the nicest way possible but leaving him looking slightly put out.

"Murdo, you have a tremendous and vivid imagination," she said pleasantly. Murdo looked slightly "put back in again" and gave a little smile.

"I need a new printer cartridge, so my suggestion is that we all go round there, right now and ask them about their cellars," continued Jessie.

A while later, after Murdo had insisted on "being tidy" and finishing the last of the rock buns, the unlikely trio trooped around the corner to Capital Computing leaving Jock sitting patiently outside the shop. Fergus was really enjoying himself. He would never have felt brave enough to take direct action like this, but he enjoyed being alongside Jessie who seemed to be an expert at taking the bull by the horns.

A young man with fair hair was stacking shelves as they went in. "Hallo, Mrs. Jenkins," he said brightly as they entered. "How's life in technoland?"

"Pretty good, Warren, thanks," said Jessie. "Those extra megs of memory you gave me seem to have made all the difference to the speed. Are there any other upgrades I should think about?"

Fergus and Murdo looked at each other with expressions that said, "What *is* she like?" Warren launched into a complex answer to Jessie's question, which left the boys' heads spinning with new vocabulary as they waited to see how Jessie would bring the conversation round to their real reason for being in the shop. Finally Warren drew his gobbledygook to a close by cheerily asking, "Anyway what can we do for you today, Mrs. J?"

"I need a new printer cartridge," she replied.

"No problem," said Warren turning to the shelf behind him and scanning the small boxes before picking one out. "Is this all you're after today?" he said waving the box and heading for the till.

"That's all, thank you, Warren, although we do have one slightly unusual query," said Jessie as she reached for her purse. "The boys and I are doing some local history research and we've been finding out about the construction of the shops on Raeburn Place and the cellars underneath them. We reckon that your cellars stretch up towards where I live, don't they?"

"You could be right, but I'm not really sure," said Warren as he began keying in the price for Jessie's new cartridge. "These cellars, or the vaults as they're called, were quite the thing when they were built, but the ones underneath here don't belong to this shop any more, they're all sealed off. One of the previous owners sold our vaults to another shop in the street fifty or sixty years ago, I think. We've only got the storerooms on ground level and no access to the vaults below the street any more."

Jessie glanced at the boys, "Really, how interesting. Do you know who bought them?"

"Couldn't tell you, Mrs. J," said Warren, "but I think it was big local news at the time for some reason. It's certainly one of the shops in this stretch that owns them, but when we bought this place last year the deeds were quite clear that the ownership of the vaults had been transferred way back. They've not been part of this shop for years."

Back at Jessie's, Murdo summed up their progress. "So we know that there are some vaults below the manhole cover but we don't know who owns them. This is a bit of a dead end. We're not really any further forward to knowing what's down there that would make our watches go backwards."

Over by the window Jessie had gone very quiet. "It's very frustrating," she said, "Stan would have known all about those vaults. He lived round here all his life and knew all the local stories. We'd be so much further on if he was here. I do feel at a loss at times."

"Can't we use your computer to try and find out a bit more, Jessie?" asked Fergus tentatively.

Jessie seemed to snap back to her usual self once again.

"Fergus, you are absolutely right," she said. "There's no point in sitting around and getting all maudlin."

So, with Jock settled in a corner of the room chewing on an old toy of Jasper's and with the boys sitting close by at either shoulder, Jessie switched on her computer and quickly went on to the internet. With her fingers in a flurry, she typed the words "Edinburgh Raeburn Place vaults local history" into the search box, and within seconds was scanning a list of results. The most promising one was a site describing itself as "Edinburgh's Local History Archive." Within that site there was an option to click on different areas of the city. Choosing "Comely Bank" led Jessie to say "Most revealing, most revealing," for the second time that day. This time the boys could see why. There was silence as all three read what had appeared on the screen.

The website that Jessie had accessed provided old newspaper articles, and the one that had come up first had the headline, "Plans Agreed for Shops on Pond." Dated 1895, the article noted that, "As part of the extension of the Comely Bank residential community this bold engineering project will involve draining the pond and building up the resulting hole to street level through the creation of a set of vaulted cellars. The final stage of construction will involve the building of a new street of shops above the vaults which will serve the growing community of Comely Bank. It will be named Raeburn Place, after the famous artist, Sir Henry Raeburn."

"Well, who would have thought that I live on top of an old pond?" said Jessie.

"Just think," said Murdo, "If they hadn't built all this we would have had a great place to play!"

"Yes, but you wouldn't have had any rock buns," noted Jessie.

"Hmm, fair point," said Murdo looking suddenly serious again.

Jessie clicked on another page, which read, "Council Leader Opens New Street." The article was dated 1898 and had the sub-heading, "Vaults Hailed an Engineering Success." There was a photo of a rather serious-looking group of bearded men in long coats beside a row of shops. The sign for Raeburn Place could just be seen above the line of their top hats. Fergus pointed out another familiar name to the others. One of the shops just visible in the corner of the picture was Crockett's Watches and Clocks.

The article described the opening of the new shopping street and the "engineering success" of the headline was the creation of the underground vaults supporting the street and the shops above. Alongside the article and the photo there was even a diagram similar to one of Jessie's plans, showing a side-on view of the street with its line of shops and then underneath the road, three tiers of archways, one on top of the other.

"It's just amazing that we are on top of all that," said Fergus.

"Does it say who owns those vaults?" asked Murdo leaning in so close to the screen that Fergus and Jessie were squeezed out.

"Well, according to the article," read Jessie, "it looks like the shops each owned the vaults below their unit. I suppose whether they used it or not depended on their business and their need for storage space."

"So why would there be manhole covers leading down to the vaults?" asked Fergus.

"There's your explanation," said Jessie, pointing to another paragraph in the article. Murdo read aloud, "Designers have responded to public concern that the draining of the pond would not be fully successful. The potential for the vaults filling with water and being a safety risk for anyone working below ground level has led to the creation of a series of quick access points to street level."

"Now," said Jessie, "what we need to find is something about the ownership of the vaults. Let's see what else we have here."

After a few more clicks of the mouse, the front page of the *Edinburgh Evening News* dated 14 August 1931 appeared on the screen. The article towards the bottom of the page had the headline, "Inventor Buys Underground Property." Jessie read aloud, "Edinburgh saw one of its more unusual property sales last week as local businessman and inventor Charles Crockett purchased six of the shop vaults underneath Raeburn Place. Local residents were bemused by the sale. One stated that "It's a bit of a white elephant," while another said "He's got more money than sense." Crockett who owns the Watches and Clocks shop on Raeburn Place was said to want the extra space for the inventions that have led to his increasingly eccentric reputation."

His face had been glued to the screen a matter of seconds before, but on reading this Murdo leapt up and disappeared. There was a loud rustling of paper from the hallway and moments later the plan from the kitchen table appeared with Murdo's legs underneath it.

"I thought we should match up the latest findings with Jessie's plan," said Murdo.

"Yes, just where is Crockett's in relation to here?" said Jessie helping Murdo to flatten out the plan on the coffee table. They found that Crockett's was situated between the Copper Kettle Café and Stein's Fish Shop. Although some way from the manhole cover, they concluded that it was possible that the six sets of vaults bought by Charles Crockett belonged to the shops between the Watches and Clocks shop and the manhole cover, including the one that now housed the cheery Warren and Capital Computing.

"Okay, so if the vaults below the manhole cover outside

here belong to Mr. Crockett then why would standing above the cellar of a clock shop make your watch go backwards?" asked Fergus.

"Well," said Murdo who had not been put off by his last explanation being cut short, "maybe the combined power of all the watches and clocks stored in Crockett's shop generates some sort of powerful collective time-force that gets channelled through the vaults and surfaces at various points around the city, and grips each watch it meets in a vice-like stranglehold that squeezes seconds out of it and ..."

Murdo looked up to find that he was alone in the living room. He could hear giggling from the hall and realized that Jessie and Fergus had sneaked out while he was in full flow. Murdo shook his head in exasperation at the fact that his good ideas seemed to be ignored so often. Fergus and Jessie then had to convince him that they were just having a bit of fun and that his idea was certainly one they would come back to, although they took care not to say when. The three then pondered on what to do next and it was Jessie who once again decided that a direct approach was the answer.

"I've been meaning to have this fixed for years," she said pointing to the wall clock with its long motionless pendulum. "I could get Bob Crockett round to look at it and we can get chatting. That way there will be no interruption from customers."

So the plan was set and Jessie made the call. She had been a customer at Crockett's for many years and the boys could hear her chatting on the phone to someone at the shop.

"He's coming tomorrow in his lunch hour," said Jessie triumphantly as she came off the phone. "Right, I think we've done all we can on the watches until tomorrow so we should get back to the cats. Let's not forget there are two mysteries to be solved here."

"We could do some brainstorming," said Murdo enthusiastically.

Fergus realized he was rolling his eyes again at the thought of more of Murdo's "blue sky thinking."

"Okay," said Jessie, spotting Fergus's reaction but forging ahead anyway. "I can't believe that so many cats can be disappearing for any natural reason. It isn't normal. I just have a hunch that someone, somewhere, is up to something."

"But who would have a grudge against cats?" said Murdo.

Jock pricked up his ears.

"A demented dog lover?" suggested Fergus.

"Someone who's allergic to cats and wants to get rid of them all?" said Murdo.

"The Society for the Protection of Garden Birds?" said Fergus.

"I don't know," pondered Jessie. "I don't think we're on the right track here."

"I suppose it depends what someone was doing with the cats," said Fergus. "We're assuming that something bad has happened to these cats."

"Yeah," said Murdo. "It could be someone who has a particular interest in cats."

"Or maybe someone is pinching them to sell them on?" said Fergus.

"Yes, maybe someone is gaining by the fact that they are going missing," said Jessie walking over to the window as if she was looking for inspiration.

"How do you mean?" said Murdo.

"Could someone profit from their disappearance?" she continued.

"Wait a minute, that's the way we have to think — is there someone or something that would benefit from cats disappearing?" said Fergus.

They all fell silent for a while and Jessie sat back down as if the moment for bright ideas had slipped by.

"Well, I'm sure the many Cat Search Agencies out there are very busy," said Murdo sarcastically. "Who on earth could profit from cats disappearing?"

"Someone trying to sell other kinds of pet?" suggested Fergus.

"That's more like it," said Jessie, "That's the way we need to think."

"So we need to find a pet shop that specializes in anything other than cats," said Murdo, being less than helpful.

"It still doesn't feel right," said Jessie. "Maybe it's not their disappearance that causes the profit. Maybe we need to think about where they are being taken, or what is happening to them when they get there."

"It's too vague ... too many what's and where's," said Murdo, getting increasingly irritated with the fact that the discussions seemed to be going nowhere.

"Well, we can't think of a good reason why someone just keeps cats away from the rest of the world, so there must be a 'what happens.' Something must be happening to those cats ... oh my poor Jasper," said Jessie, momentarily distracted at the thought of what might be happening to her cat.

"But what could anyone be doing with dozens of cats?" asked Murdo, beginning to go red in the face with frustration. "Playing with a giant ball of wool?"

"Are you going to come up with any useful ideas today?" asked Fergus. Murdo looked like he might begin to sulk.

"Cats don't do that much other than eat, sleep and play about a bit," said Murdo defensively, "So what on earth can someone be doing with them that makes a profit?"

"Okay then," said Fergus deciding to act as a peacemaker before Murdo's impatience got the better of him. "Let's agree with Murdo. Whoever is taking the cats isn't doing it just to play with them, and you can't make much money out of a sleeping cat, so that just leaves eating."

"CAT FOOD!"

The boys jumped as Jessie shot to her feet far quicker than anyone of her age should try to do. "Cat food!" she shouted again, looking at the boys with a wild glint in her eyes and not seeming to have suffered any ill effects from her sudden movement.

"Jessie, have we ever told you that it's a bad habit to shout out random words without explanation?" said Murdo, his pulse beginning to slow again after the shock of the shout.

Jessie ignored the comment and began to pace with a slight limp around the room, her cardigan flapping as she went. "You see, you've cracked it. Murdo's right — all cats do is eat, sleep and play about a bit. Fergus is right too. No one can make any money from sleeping and playing cats. So the only thing left is "eating." What do cats eat? Cat food! It must be big business judging by the number of adverts on the telly."

"So what are you getting at?" said Murdo, liking Jessie's train of thought so far, but not seeing quite what station it was about to arrive at.

"I don't know, I don't know, but this feels right," said Jessie sinking back into her armchair again, frustrated that they had hit another dead end. "Someone must know what kind of food cats like. Maybe that would help us move this along a bit."

"Wait a minute!" This time it was Fergus. He was sitting bolt upright on the settee with a fiery purpose in his eyes. The next second he leapt up, vaulted the coffee table and sat at the computer, clicking on the mouse.

"Jessie is right, someone does know what kind of food cats like," said Fergus firmly as he clicked into an internet search engine.

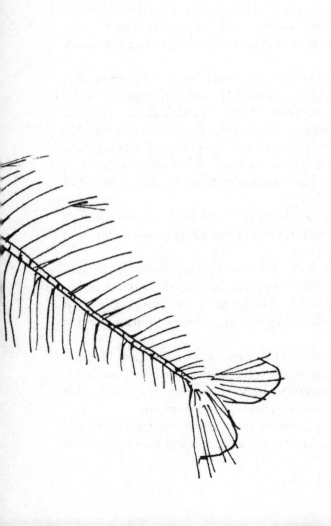

7. Prime Suspect

"Here we are," said Fergus.

Murdo and Jessie were standing behind him, looking at the computer screen. Fergus had run a search on "Cats and Edinburgh" to reveal the results they had looked at a few days before. He clicked on the fourth option and the screen changed.

"Well, well, well," murmured Jessie, "that is a development. Well remembered, Fergus."

Murdo read the screen aloud. "Study into the Formation of Feline Eating Habits, University of Edinburgh, 1995, Dissertation by Davidson Stein."

"I knew we'd seen something about cats and eating before," said Fergus. "Maybe this will tell us something about why cats like certain foods."

Fergus went into the research project file and scrolled through the numerous pages of the document. It was solid text with the occasional graph or table of numbers. "Wow, this has nearly put me to sleep already it's so boring," said Fergus, disappointment creeping into his voice.

Headings like "Taste Formation in the Juvenile Cat" and "Personality and Preference Development in the Maturing Cat," were highlighted in bold as Fergus scrolled through the document trying to find something that looked easy to read.

"Try going to the end to find the Conclusion," suggested Jessie.

Fergus tried this but ended up in something called a bibliography.

"List of books," explained Jessie.

"So I see," said Fergus going back up the list of authors and journals to the top of a Conclusions paragraph.

"Right, what does our friend, Davidson, conclude?" asked Jessie leaning into the screen again.

"Cats are very particular about their choice of food," read Murdo. "Blah, blah, blah. The preference for particular tastes is formed at a very young age, namely in the first three to six months.

"Well, I think we may be heading in the wrong direction. Cats form their eating habits young and it's not kittens that are disappearing, it's cats of all ages. According to this they would all have decided what food they like long ago."

"My Jasper is certainly no spring chicken," said Jessie, "But there's something about this idea. I like it."

"Just imagine if someone cornered the cat food market. How much would that be worth?" said Fergus.

"Millions?" speculated Murdo.

"Billions?" added Jessie.

"Gazillions," said Fergus emphatically. "Imagine if someone could make sure that cats only liked one brand of cat food. They would be laughing all the way to the bank."

"So," said Murdo joining in on the act, "All you would have to do would be to kidnap loads of cats and somehow convince them that eating one brand of cat food was the thing to do. Maybe it's hypnosis. Can animals be hypnotized?"

For the first time that day Murdo's idea was taken seriously by Fergus and Jessie, who both nodded at the possibilities that his question had posed.

"So where do we go from here?" asked Murdo.

"Let's find out if there are any cat food suppliers or manufacturers in Edinburgh," said Jessie.

Fergus went back to the search screen and typed "cat food," "Edinburgh" and "suppliers."

Some of the same answers came up as before, but so did two company names, Kitty Kitchen and Petfood Products.

Fergus clicked on "Kitty Kitchen" and Murdo read out, "'Specialist food for your special friend.' Pee-uke." The wording on the website went on to be as pink and flowery as the site itself.

"I think we've got the gist of that," said Jessie. "Try the other one."

Petfood Products had a much more technical looking website. "Nine Lives: Cat Food for the 21st Century," read Murdo. "A diet for the modern cat — Internet sales and delivery — Service to be launched this autumn." There was only an email address for those wishing to receive an information mailing on the cat food. Jessie leaned over Fergus and quickly typed, "I am interested in further information on your products and services. Please send details by return. With thanks, Mrs. J. Jenkins."

Their internet activity was interrupted by the phone ringing and Fergus suddenly realized that time had flown by with all of the morning's activities. Sure enough his mum was checking that everything was okay and that the boys weren't getting in Jessie's way. "They are no problem at all, Fiona, although I'll send them back up the hill shortly as I've promised a friend I'll help her with something this afternoon," said Jessie.

As Jessie hung up, two bleeps announced that messages had arrived in her inbox. Firstly there was a reply from Precision Customer Services noting that they had received no other reports of DataBoys going backwards and recommending returning the malfunctioning watch to the shop it was purchased from, as the first step towards diagnosis and repair. "Well, no great surprise there," said Jessie deleting the response.

The other email was an automated response, which noted that Jessie had now been added to the customer mailing list for Nine Lives, which would be launched at the end of the month, when more details would follow.

The next morning the boys were once again at Jessie's, this time finishing off inputting the information gathered by Murdo into the database. Murdo read out the details from his big folder of lost cat posters as Fergus typed them in. This gave them a welcome distraction from the eagerly anticipated appointment with Mr. Crockett. While they worked away, Jessie sat in her armchair reading Murdo's diary of the investigation, although the boys soon spotted that she had not only fallen asleep while doing so but was snoring deeply.

"Oh dear, I'm sure we told her it would be an interesting read," said Fergus.

"I'm very concerned she's not taking this seriously enough," said Murdo. "If she starts drooling on that diary I will not be happy," he added.

As the boys keyed in the last entry, a shadowy figure appeared through the net curtains and at precisely one o'clock the doorbell rang.

Jessie sat up as if she'd been electrocuted. "What?!.. Oh dear, oh my goodness ... is that the time? ... Must have dozed off ... Boys, you should have woken me ... Dear me, dear me." She eased herself out of her chair and walked stiffly to the front door.

The boys could hear a man's voice as Jessie led the visitor into the hall. "Not at all, Mrs. Jenkins — I remember you mentioning this clock before."

"I've got two of my friends here at the moment," said Jessie as she entered the living room. She was followed by a small, round man who was using a comb to move an invisible strand of hair over his gleaming bald head.

"Fergus and Murdo, this is Mr. Crockett," said Jessie.

"Ah the DataBoy," said Mr. Crockett, pocketing the comb, the buttons on his jacket straining as he did so. Fergus raised his eyebrows in surprise at the shop owner's ability to remember his customers.

"Has it been as good as you hoped, young man?" he asked, leaning towards Fergus, his eyeballs magnified by his thick round glasses.

Fergus resisted the temptation to say, "Yes, apart from the times it goes backwards when I'm standing on the manhole cover outside." That wasn't part of the planned script for this stage of the investigation and he kept his answer to a polite "yes thanks" instead.

"So let's have a look at this then," said Mr. Crockett who had spotted the clock on the wall by the fireplace and bustled over to look at it. He had to stand on tiptoes to peer into the workings, which the open sides of the clock casing revealed.

"It's not worked for years," said Jessie. "My husband actually bought it at your shop but long before you would remember. I think it might have been your grandfather who was in the shop at the time."

"Ah, the great inventor," said Mr. Crockett with a thin smile as he produced a tiny brush from his pocket and dusted carefully at the exposed cogs.

"We've been doing a local history project," chipped in Murdo, "and we read about him in some old newspapers. Did he ever invent anything useful?"

Still peering into the clock, Mr. Crockett gave a short clipped laugh as he continued to investigate the mechanism. "He would say so, but nothing has exactly become a household object." Distracted momentarily from the timepiece, Mr Crockett removed his glasses to polish them with a large, white hanky. As soon as he replaced them his eyeballs zoomed back to giant size. "Let me see, what were some of his better efforts?" he said. "The telescopic table leg, the vibrating mixing bowl, the spring-loaded bookends and the marmalade dispensing gun. They're not exactly as famous as the microwave oven or the telephone are they?" he said, turning his attention back to the insides of the wall clock.

"Is it true that he bought vaults from other shops for all of his inventions?" asked Fergus.

"Yes, that's right," said Mr. Crockett, his eyebrows rising up his shiny forehead in surprise at Fergus's level of knowledge. "He bought the vaults from about half a dozen shops I think, and then filled the space with all sorts of junk. I expect my grandmother was quite pleased that it wasn't in the house any more."

"So what do you use all that space for now?" asked Jessie innocently.

"Well, we only use a little for storage and we lease the rest to our neighbours," said Mr. Crockett. "I didn't carry on my grandfather's inventing habits so we don't have much need for those rooms."

The boys looked at each other, both thinking back to the list of shops they had built up which would tell them who Mr. Crockett's neighbours were.

"The Copper Kettle?" said Murdo quickly.

"I'm sorry?" said Mr. Crockett momentarily confused.

"You said you leased the vaults to your neighbours," said Murdo, trying not to sound too anxious for an answer. "Isn't that the Copper Kettle Café?"

"Oh no, the other side," said Mr. Crockett. "My grandfather was probably turning in his grave as I signed the papers, but they wanted the extra space for big freezers and things like that."

"Who's on the other side?" said Jessie.

"The Fish Shop," said Mr. Crockett and Fergus at the same time.

"Yes, the owner there and myself are both in the unusual position of taking on our grandfathers' businesses," said Mr. Crockett.

"Who's the owner now?" asked Jessie.

"Davidson," said Mr. Crockett. "Davidson Stein."

Ten minutes had passed since Mr. Crockett had left, saying that he would need to order some parts in order to repair Jessie's clock. There was still a state of high excitement in Jessie's living room. Fergus wondered how he had ever thought that this room seemed old and dusty because there was now a buzz about the place. As he thought back to the clock shop manager's visit, he wondered if Mr. Crockett had noticed that they suddenly didn't seem interested in Jessie's damaged clock. As soon as he had mentioned that the vaults were leased by a man who was an expert in cats' eating habits, they had all had difficulty concentrating. Once Jessie had closed the door on the departing Mr. Crockett, Murdo went into overdrive with theories about what a fish shop might want with the vaults under Raeburn Place.

"Just how much storage space does a fish shop need?" asked Murdo, pacing up and down the living room. "Six vaults? Six vaults? You could fit a lot of cats in six vaults you know. A lot more than forty-four," he said, picking up and waving his file.

"We started asking about the vaults because of the watches, but we've ended up with something that points to the cats. Could there be a link between the investigations? Why would missing cats make watches go backwards? It's not making sense!"

Murdo's brow was furrowing so deeply that Fergus began to get concerned that he would do himself some permanent damage and decided it was time to change tack.

"What do you know about Stein's Fish Shop, Jessie?" asked Fergus. "You've lived here the longest."

"Well, I have, but I can't really help you," said Jessie. "Stan hated fish, you see, so if there's one shop that I've not been into in Raeburn Place in all my years in Comely Bank, it's Stein's."

"Mum buys our fish at the supermarket so we've never been in either," said Fergus.

"Our prime suspect, the one shop that we need information on and our local sources have drawn a blank!" Murdo slapped his hand to his forehead. "Well, we'll have to find out about it if we want to go any further at all. If only we could do things properly and pull Davidson Stein in for questioning," said Murdo thumping a pudgy fist into the palm of his other hand.

"Well, we could do another thing that often happens when you have a suspect," said Jessie. "I think it might be time for you to stake out Mr. Stein's."

Murdo stopped in his tracks and a grin split his large face. Fergus thought that he could hear Murdo's brain whirring into action.

8. The Stakeout

Murdo's plans for the stakeout involved as many different ways of being close to the shop at different times of the day as possible and over the next few days the boys got to know Raeburn Place very well in their efforts to learn more about Stein's the Fishmongers. They spent as much time as near to the shop as they could, without making it too obvious that they were doing so. They walked past on the other side of the road together, they cycled past individually, they pretended to bump into each other outside the shop and they had conversations looking over each other's shoulders. Jock got quite frustrated with it all as what he thought was going to be a decent walk never seemed to turn into one.

Jessie was in on the stakeout as well. She was rediscovering a few recipes having missed out on fish dishes for years. She went into the shop three times during the week and struck up conversations with the staff as she bought a variety of seafood. By the end of the week she concluded that the shop sold excellent fish. The only problem she had encountered was a paper clip accidentally wrapped up with a piece of cod that she had bought. "I could have choked on that!" she said brandishing the paper clip, which she had since filed in her cardigan pocket. "Still the cod was rather good," she added. Fergus found himself hoping that Jessie hadn't filed the bones away in her pocket for future reference too.

Spurred on by Jessie's efforts, Fergus couldn't resist the temptation to go inside the shop too, but he knew that he had made his mum slightly suspicious by suggesting that

89

they ate a fish dish and then offering to go and buy the chief ingredient.

"Why the sudden liking for fish?" asked his mum.

"Come on, Mum, it's good for you. You should eat what's put in front of you," said Fergus with an impish smile.

Jessie had instructed the boys to "switch on their beady eyes" for the week, so they did their best to concentrate hard each day. Murdo even set the alarm on his DataBoy to bleep every hour, at which point he summarized the previous sixty minutes' activity in a new notebook bought specially for the stakeout. After several days the three investigators had deduced that there were four main people in the shop.

There was a large and fearsome woman who served behind the counter. Murdo began describing her in his notebook as "Beetroot" because of the colour of her face. Fergus had found her rather scary when he had gone into the shop, realizing quickly that she had little patience if you didn't know exactly what you wanted. Even Jessie, who the boys would have thought could have chatted to anyone, came back talking about Beetroot. "I think these days they would say that she did not possess the people-skills required of a customer service position."

During the week Beetroot was helped occasionally by a lanky man with a whiskery chin and a long sharp nose, which Murdo thought looked like a runner bean, a vegetable that he particularly disliked. "Beanface," as the man became known, seemed to spend most of his time carrying large boxes around and bringing fish through to the counter from the back of the shop. The boys had also seen him driving a white van to and from an archway a few doors along from the shop. On investigating more closely they found that this led to a lane and courtyard behind the shop.

Fergus, Jessie and Murdo had seen much less of the other two people, but it was these men who they all agreed that they wanted to know more about.

The straight-backed, dark-haired, suited man with the goatee beard had all the hallmarks of being the boss, as he was only occasionally near the front of the shop and was too smartly dressed to spend any length of time near the smells and splashes of a working fishmonger. Fergus described him as the "least likely-looking person to manage a fish shop." He was usually seen coming and going in an unnaturally shiny blue four-wheel drive with the registration plate "STE 1 N." They all decided from Day One that this was Davidson Stein.

The final one of the four was the biggest mystery. By the end of the week they didn't know his name and had no idea what he did. Murdo called him "Cogs." "He's doing all of his work behind the scenes," he said explaining his choice of name. Sure enough, Murdo's notebook revealed that the bespectacled young man usually arrived early each day and left promptly at 5pm but was never seen around the shop area. The only other daily sighting was when he nipped out for a sandwich at lunchtime, which he sometimes ate while reading a book in the park. Rather confusingly, at the end of Day Three Cogs didn't seem to leave the shop or appear the next morning, but at the end of Day Four he emerged as if he had been there all along. The boys were convinced that the stakeout had been thorough but either Cogs had arrived particularly early and left particularly late on Day Three, or he had spent the night in the shop, which they agreed was too bizarre to be possible.

The three concluded that they had built up as much of a picture as they could from the stakeout, and that they had all bought as much fish as was possible in such a short period of time without seeming suspicious.

Murdo had put forward a strong case that the natural

next step should involve trying to find out more about Cogs, simply by following him at the end of a working day. This was partly because he was the one they knew least about, but also because he was the only one who left the shop on foot, as Stein swished away in his four-wheel drive, Beanface roared off in the white van and Beetroot was collected by an equally beetroot-coloured and equally large man in a sagging rusty car.

Jessie was only happy with this proposal on three conditions. The first was that the boys would go no further than their parents would normally allow. The second was that they borrowed her old mobile phone, Jessie having just upgraded to a new, slim and silvery one the day before. The boys had to promise her to call at the first hint of a problem. The third was that they had to swear solemnly that they would not climb any walls or try to get into anyone's garden.

"I don't think that jumping on walls is Cogs's style," said Murdo defensively.

Jessie replied that she didn't know what his style was, but if it involved scaling any vertical structures the boys were not to follow him.

And so the boys and Jock took up position in the bus shelter close to Stein's Fish Shop waiting for Cogs to emerge, but found that he was taking longer than they had bargained for. Fortunately, Murdo had brought some entertainment along in his rucksack but after half an hour of hangman and a game of travel chess, they were once again at a loose end.

"Let's call Jessie," said Murdo and they used her phone to check in and tell her that there was no progress as yet.

"I bet your sister would be impressed with Jessie's new phone," said Fergus.

"Yeah, she'd be dead jealous," said Murdo with a grin. He then looked thoughtful and said, "Actually we could have a bit of fun here."

Murdo quickly opened Jessie's old phone again, checked the memory function of his DataBoy for a phone number and began to text. Fergus leaned over his shoulder for a better view.

Murdo keyed in "Hi how r u" and pressed "send." Within a minute the phone bleeped and the reply "Who r u?" popped up on the mobile's tiny screen.

"A secret admirer," texted Murdo giggling. Again there was a short delay and the response "give me a name."

"What name shall I put?" said Murdo.

"Who does she really like?" asked Fergus.

"A boy at school called Danny MacKay," said Murdo sticking two fingers down his throat and pretending to gag. He returned to his texting and keyed in "Danny M" and after a pause added "I think u r really cool."

This time the phone bleeped faster than it had done before. Murdo chuckled as he read it and held the phone up so that Fergus could see it.

"I think u r gr8" was the message.

"It's not often my sister has said that to me," said Murdo with a smile. "I should frame it!" Then he looked suddenly serious. "I will be in *so* much trouble if she ever finds out that was me."

Suddenly the boys were distracted. The white van pulled out from the archway and roared past them with Beanface at the wheel.

"Right, back to business. We'd better concentrate. There's no point being on a stakeout and not progressing the investigation."

Fergus smiled to himself as the business-like Murdo returned. It was just in time because as Murdo put the phone away Cogs appeared at the shop door.

"Let him get as far as the Post Office before we start following," said Murdo.

Cogs headed down Raeburn Place, walking briskly and adjusting the weight of a black bag over one shoulder.

"That's a bag for a laptop," said Murdo. "Dad has one of those."

"Why's he got one of those? I can't imagine they're much use when you're filleting fish," said Fergus. "Come on, we'd better go."

Cogs reached the Post Office and continued to walk away from the fish shop. The boys soon found that following him wasn't too difficult and the only time they began to worry was when the young man looked around three times in quick succession. At first they thought that he had noticed that he was being followed, but after a moment's panic they realized that he was just checking whether or not a bus was coming as he approached a bus stop. He paused briefly at the stop but then decided not to bother, and set off again with the boys walking about thirty metres behind. Jock was happy as they seemed to be going a bit further than any other day that week.

Eventually, they approached a residential area where other pedestrians had dwindled to one or two. The boys were feeling a bit more exposed as they continued to follow at what they felt was a safe distance. They began to hang back a bit more, but then disaster struck. Cogs rounded a corner and when the boys reached it, he had gone.

"No way!" said Murdo disbelievingly

"He's vanished," said Fergus looking around. The sign above told them that they were in Nelson Street but all that it had to offer were rows of closed doors. The boys looked up at a series of blank windows, trying to spot movement in one of the flats that would show them that someone had just returned home. They gave nothing away except reflections of the buildings on the other side of the road.

"I can't believe we had him all that way and then lost him!" said Murdo.

"At least we know this street has some sort of connection," said Fergus trying to find something positive out of this frustrating situation.

Suddenly the red front door of number 10 opened and a young woman came out. She walked briskly down the steps to the pavement and headed straight for a sporty bottle-green Mazda. As she unlocked the car she placed a laptop bag on the passenger seat. She climbed in, started the engine and accelerated away quickly.

"That was the same bag," said Fergus. "There was a grey stripe on the side and a buckle hanging off."

"Unfortunately, I wasn't sharp enough to get the car registration though," said Murdo.

"MM2," said Fergus. "Personalized number plate."

"I am reminded at times why it is useful having you around," Murdo nodded, as he checked his watch and scribbled these new facts in his notebook.

At that moment a head appeared at the boys' feet. Jock barked a friendly "hallo." A man had come upstairs from a basement flat and was now level with the pavement where the boys were standing.

"Afternoon, boys," he said. "You look lost, can I help?"

"No we're ...," started Murdo.

"Doing a treasure hunt," finished Fergus quickly.

Murdo looked at Fergus with a blank expression.

"Yes," said Fergus pointing at Murdo's notebook. "We ... er ... need the names of the residents of Number 10 Nelson Street. This is Nelson Street, isn't it?" he said vaguely.

Murdo joined in the act and waved his notebook as if they had been collecting Treasure Hunt answers all day.

"Well," said the man, "The names are on the buzzer, so that's easy enough for you."

"Who's who though? asked Fergus anxiously. "Who lives on which floor?"

"Well, I can help you there," said the man. "Paul Lomax

is on the top floor. The Traynor family are in the middle. Those are their kids' bikes against the railings, and Mrs. Connor lives on the ground floor. Then there's me, Philip Thomas, in the basement."

"Is Paul Lomax the guy with the glasses and the laptop bag?" asked Fergus, trying to sound like he was just making polite conversation.

"Yes, he's some sort of computer whizz," said Mr. Thomas. "He was a student until last year but seems to have landed a good job. I suppose it's the profession to be in these days. So are you going to get a prize?" asked the man.

"Sorry?" said Fergus.

"For the Treasure Hunt," said Mr. Thomas, pointing to Murdo's notebook.

"Certainly hope so," said Murdo. "Come on, Fergus, we'd better go! Thanks for your help," he called as they set off.

"We're getting good at this," said Fergus out of the corner of his mouth as they turned and headed back towards Comely Bank. Murdo nodded as he pressed the "dial" button on Jessie's mobile.

"Just reporting in," he said importantly. "We're heading back to base with important new information."

"So they've got a computer guy working in a Fish Shop — what is that all about?" said Jessie thoughtfully as the boys sipped juice in her front room.

"Tell me about the car again."

"It was very flash," said Murdo.

"It was a Mazda," said Fergus.

"And who was driving?" asked Jessie.

"She was as flash as the car," said Murdo.

"Dark hair — short, dark glasses — wraparound, dark jacket — leather," said Fergus.

"This guy is good," said Jessie looking at Murdo and nodding sideways at Fergus.

"That's why I took him on," said Murdo seriously.

"Heh, I took you on!" Fergus protested.

"I thought I'd taken both of you on!" said Jessie with a smile. "Now boys, that was a good piece of work today. I've been thinking about the next step. We need a way in. We need to get into the back of the fish shop."

"We could break in at night!" said Murdo with a flourish of his fist, his eyes brightening with the thought of planning another escapade. "We'll get some wire, pick the lock on the back door of the shop, then disable any alarms and put the guard dogs to sleep with some drugged meat. We'll tie up any security guards, tape their mouths and then we'll start the search with our headtorches on ..."

"Boys," said Jessie firmly. "There are times when I shall be pulling rank because of my age. Now is one of those times. We will *not* be involved in any illegal activities. We have enough intelligence between the three of us, four including Jock, not to have to resort to that sort of behaviour. Murdo, I appreciate your enthusiasm but I do not want to have to visit you in prison and start planning ways of breaking you out instead of breaking in."

Murdo looked like he was beginning to wish he had chosen two other words than "break" and "in." Fergus kept quiet, secretly relieved that there would be no more break-in attempts to add to their efforts at the manhole cover a few days before.

"Well, we can get into the front part of the shop easily enough, but how do we get beyond the counter?" said Murdo trying to restore some credibility.

"You need to work there," reasoned Fergus.

"Or have some reason to go to the back of the shop, like for some sort of meeting, for example," mused Jessie.

"So we need a way to get two boys, a dog and an old woman to a meeting in a fish shop," said Murdo. He suddenly realized what he had just called Jessie and went bright pink.

"That's all right , Murdo," said Jessie, "I am old and I'm a woman. Just don't feel that you have to remind me too often."

"How old are you?" said Murdo trying to make polite conversation and failing miserably. He promptly went even pinker. "Er ... I'm sorry, Jessie ..."

"Let's just say I'm old enough to be wise enough not to let being old enough to be wise enough concern me," said Jessie.

Fergus had to scrunch up his eyes and squidge his brain around a bit to make sense of what Jessie had said, but he got there eventually. Meanwhile, Murdo looked rather blank but smiled, relieved that he had succeeded in remaining on friendly terms with Jessie after almost offending her twice in one minute.

"Now ... where were we?" Jessie said with a wink at Fergus. "Why *would* two boys, a dog and an old woman want to have a meeting in a fish shop?"

"I can't see why two boys and a dog would have a meeting there, but I can see why a *woman* might," said Fergus who had been pondering on this. Jessie and Murdo looked at him expectantly.

"To make a complaint," he said. "My mum's always writing letters of complaint and sometimes in shops she'll ask to see the manager. It's *so* embarrassing."

"So simple and yet so brilliant," said Jessie nodding enthusiastically. She rummaged in her cardigan pocket and held up the paper clip that she had found with her fish. "Boys, I give you Exhibit A. A perfect reason to ask to see the manager and get beyond the counter." She looked thoughtful for a moment. "The only problem is that in doing it that way you're not getting a chance for a quick look around."

Murdo looked like he was itching to point out that his

idea of breaking-in would have provided them with plenty of opportunities to look around without being seen.

"I think we're on the right track," said Jessie. "Okay, so here's the story so far. A woman makes a complaint and asks to see the manager. What happens next?"

"The manager asks the woman into his office to discuss the matter?" said Fergus.

"The manager listens patiently to the woman making her complaint," said Murdo picking up the story.

"The manager has to leave the office for a few minutes leaving the woman on her own to prowl around," said Fergus sounding a bit uncertain and feeling like he had skipped a few lines.

"Why *does* the manager leave the office?" said Jessie spotting the gap in Fergus's story.

"The toilet!" said Murdo jumping up.

"It's just at the end of the hall," said Jessie with a smile and another wink to Fergus.

"No!" said Murdo in frustration sitting down again. "The manager leaves the office because he needs the toilet!"

Fergus looked perplexed, "How exactly do we plan a meeting to coincide with the manager needing to go to the loo?"

"We could slip something into his tea that makes him need to go!" said Murdo excitedly.

"How do we know he's going to have a cup of tea? Do we take a flask in with us?" asked Fergus in exasperation.

"Boys, boys, we might be investigators but we're not quite MI5," said Jessie. "Whilst we're still operating in Comely Bank I think we'll avoid drugging people's hot drinks and save those tactics for when we move into international espionage. Now why does the manager leave the office?" Jessie repeated.

Murdo's eyes flashed as he fired suggestions off like a machine gun. "He might go to fetch something, to feed his parking meter, to put the kettle on or to get a glass of water for the woman who's now feeling faint?"

Fergus began to suspect that Jessie had an answer up her sleeve.

"Because he's suddenly needed elsewhere," said Fergus.

"Exactly," said Jessie.

"Why's he needed elsewhere?" said Murdo.

"Because two boys and a dog are creating an almighty disturbance in the shop," said Jessie.

Jock growled, barked and began to spin round in a circle chasing his tail.

"Exactly, Jock," said Jessie.

9. Operation Paper Clip

The hatching of the plan to get inside the fish shop was done in Jessie's living room and involved her preparing a short speech, the boys speculating on the actions of the fish shop staff and then synchronizing their DataBoys with Stan's old watch.

"Timing is everything in this next stage of the campaign, boys. You must play your part at exactly the right time for things to work out," Jessie said, as she tucked Stan's watch into her cardigan pocket.

The next day had been chosen to put the plan into action and the boys were in position early, once again loitering at the bus stop just far enough away from the fish shop to see but be unseen. Jock sat quietly having seemingly accepted the bus shelter as some new kind of home. The boys had already noted the arrival of Beetroot and Beanface and the subsequent opening of the shop, and as soon as they saw Stein's four-wheel-drive sweeping through the archway to the back of the shop thirty minutes later, they called Jessie to start the thirty minute countdown of what Murdo had called "Operation Paper Clip."

Twenty-nine minutes and three seconds later, according to the stopwatch on Fergus's DataBoy, the boys saw Jessie coming into view, limping slightly as she headed purposefully along Raeburn Place towards the shops.

"Does she ever wear anything else?" asked Murdo, noting that once again Jessie's pink cardigan was her fashion statement for the day.

"Why would she?" said Fergus. "She has everything she needs in those pockets."

The boys watched her march up to the fish shop and head in without hesitation or even a glance in their direction.

"What a professional," murmured Murdo nodding appreciatively.

Unfortunately if Murdo had seen what happened next he might have changed his opinion. Things started smoothly enough as Jessie strode up to the counter and asked to see the manager of the shop, announcing that she had a matter of complaint, which she was only prepared to discuss with him. Beetroot looked distinctly unimpressed at this request, her face scrunching up as if she had been swatted on the nose with a bunch of nettles, but with a grunt of disapproval she wheeled round and went to the back of the shop.

It was then that despite all of the planning and practising, Jessie found herself momentarily floundering. Stein emerged from the back of the shop and politely offered her the chance to follow him to his office, behaving exactly as their plan anticipated he would in his efforts to preserve good customer relations. It was as Stein ushered Jessie behind the counter along the corridor and into his office, that Jessie found herself in a panic. She simply hadn't thought of who she was going to be for the next few minutes and being Mrs. Jenkins suddenly didn't seem like a good idea.

"Please do come through this way Mrs. ...?"

"Sprockett," Jessie blurted, surprising herself with how quickly she produced a false name and immediately regretting the fact that she had come up with such a ridiculous one.

"Mrs. ... Sprockett, I am so sorry to hear that you've had cause to complain," Stein said smoothly. "Now tell me all about it and we'll see what we can do," he continued, showing Jessie to a chair and walking around his neat desk. Jessie took her time to settle into the seat to give herself the chance to recover from having to think on her feet. She noticed how Stein's goatee beard was so neat that every hair looked as though it had been individually positioned. Stein sat down opposite her, a wall of books and folders on the shelves behind him, and smoothed out an invisible wrinkle in his dark suit. He placed his hands together, his perfectly manicured fingers pointing upwards and gave Jessie what she reckoned was probably his most winning smile. With his mouth forced up at the corners giving a glimpse of gleaming teeth, Stein looked like a fox who had just eaten a shed full of chickens.

"Now," said Stein, "how can I help?"

"It's a simple enough story," said Jessie picking up on the plan once again. "I purchased some fish recently from your shop and found this in it." Jessie produced the paper clip and held it up with a flourish.

"Well," said Stein taking the offending article and examining it carefully like a scientist examining a small insect. "That is most unusual, and of course highly irregular. I would be happy to offer you both my fullest apology and some appropriate compensation. Please tell me exactly when this took place." Stein's expression had changed to one of concern, his forehead crumpled into a deliberate frown.

Jessie began to explain in more detail when she had purchased the fish, knowing that if the plan went smoothly she wouldn't have to get too far into her story. She did her best to continue speaking as the first of some muffled sounds and raised voices could be heard through the closed door of the office. Stein's steely blue eyes flickered momentarily as he registered the disturbance outside, but he continued to give Jessie his full attention, until the barking started. Jessie knew that they were now three and a half minutes into this stage of the plan and Jock was beginning to play his part. Just as they had hoped, the sound of an increasingly agitated dog in the shop was too much for Stein to ignore.

"Please excuse me for one moment, Mrs. Sprockett," he said, still smiling as he slipped off his seat and around the desk to the door. "This doesn't sound quite like a normal morning."

Stein left the room leaving the door half open. Jessie quickly and quietly pushed the door a little further shut, and turned to look at the office with a glint of determination. It was time for *her* to switch on her own beady eyes.

Stein's desk was terrifyingly tidy. Even the paper clips appeared to have been counted, polished and individually placed. The documents on his desk were neatly set out like a display rather than a working office, but from what Jessie could see of the titles, they were all related disappointingly to the business of managing a fish shop.

Moving behind Stein's desk she looked along the names on the folders, files and books, which formed the wall behind. She spotted the titles *Invoices, Three Year Business Plan* and *The Entrepreneur's Encyclopaedia* in her first glance.

The barking could still be heard although Jessie kept glancing back at the door to make sure she was safe. As she did so, a splash of colour caught her eye. She looked more closely at the photo frame on the desk that had attracted her attention. The picture was of a dark-haired woman in sunglasses perched on the bonnet of a green sports car. The registration "MM2" was just visible.

"Well, well, well," said Jessie.

She turned her attention back to the bookshelf and continued scanning the contents, running a finger along the spines of the books as she did so. All the way along the titles seemed to relate to running small businesses or to the fish industry, until Jessie's eye was drawn to one which seemed different. "*Total Recall* by Maxine McDermott," said Jessie quietly, "M. M.? I wonder." Jessie threw half a glance back to the photo on the desk and slid the book from the shelf, flicking the back cover open as she did so to reveal a short paragraph on the author along with a photo.

"Dark hair — short, dark glasses — wraparound, dark jacket — leather. Bingo!" said Jessie quietly. Jessie slid the book back onto the shelf and turned her attention to Stein's desk, quietly opening the top drawer. At the top was a small tray neatly stocked with staples, drawing pins and paper clips. The only thing that seemed out of place was a short length of black wire with a microphone on the end. "Has that been cut or was it chopped in half by a falling drain cover I wonder?" thought Jessie to herself.

"Interesting, very interesting," she said quietly moving the tray aside to look at the files stored in the drawer. The first one was entitled "The Chamber — Technical Specifications." At the sight of the next one Jessie froze, her head in a spin. She began to pull out the folder marked "Nine Lives — Launch Plans" when she heard footsteps and suddenly realized that she had been distracted enough not to notice the barking coming to an end. Shoving the file back in she shut the drawer quickly and turned to get back to her seat, but as she did so she felt a pull at her arm. She continued to her seat tugging as she went before looking round to find that a thread of wool from the sleeve of her pink cardigan had snagged on the drawer and stuck in it as it had closed. She could hear Stein just a few steps away and there was no time to release it. Jessie lunged back to her seat just before the door opened, the thread of wool unravelling from her sleeve even further as she did so. As Davidson Stein strode back into the room, the long pink thread still connected her cardigan with the top drawer of his desk. Fortunately for Jessie, Stein walked around the other side of the desk and the distraction of the situation in the shop continued to take his attention as he sat back in his black leather swivel chair.

"My apologies, Mrs. Sprockett. What a ridiculous situation. Two boys completely unable to control their irritating little dog in the middle of my shop."

"Oh dear," said Jessie trying to sound sympathetic as she tried as subtly as she could to tug on the thread without Stein noticing. It was no good. It was stuck fast.

"Never mind," said Stein shaking his head briskly and making a precise note to himself on an otherwise blank sheet of paper. "One of my staff will do some follow-up work there and ensure that there is no such behaviour again. Young people today are out of control."

"Isn't it people of my generation that are supposed to say things like that?" said Jessie, trying to sound relaxed, as she again masked the fact that she was tugging as hard as she could on the tight pink thread leading from her sleeve right around Stein's polished desk.

Stein managed a short clipped laugh. "Mrs. Sprockett, I can only apologize. I have been distracted from your distressing situation. Please do accept my sincere apologies and this voucher," he said writing on a compliments slip with a flourish of a fountain pen. Jessie took the slip awkwardly, covering up the problem with her cardigan as she leaned forward. "Exchange for goods to the value of £20," she read out, "Well, thank you for taking my complaint so seriously," she said starting to feel bad that she was being rewarded for snooping around his office.

Jessie was rapidly running out of reasons for remaining

in Stein's office and desperately needed some delaying tactics until she could free herself. "That's a lovely photo," she said nodding at the frame on his desk. "Is that your wife?"

As soon as Jessie had asked the question she knew that she had made a mistake. It felt like a chill had descended on the room. "It's very clever of you to see the photo from where you're sitting," said Stein quietly. His eyes appeared to darken and his gaze sharpened.

"I can never resist looking at a photo," said Jessie trying to make light of the situation.

"Did you resist the chance to look at much more while I was out of the room?" said Stein, his eyes flitting around his office to find anything out of place.

"Mr. Stein, I don't like what you are insinuating," said Jessie trying to sound like an insulted old lady even though she knew that she was really in the wrong and had been found out.

Stein looked down to where Jessie's pink cardigan was attached to his desk. He calmly opened the top drawer, freed the thread and began to neatly roll it around two fingers. Stein now assumed the manner of a prosecutor in a courtroom who has just made a breakthrough with a chief suspect. "Mrs. ... eh ... Sprockett," he said in a deliberate way that suggested that he now didn't for a minute think that "Sprockett" was Jessie's real name. "You must forgive me ... boys, dogs, wandering ladies with x-ray vision in the same morning ... I hardly know which way to turn today."

Stein stood up and walked around his desk. He handed Jessie the little ball of wool with one hand while with the other he reached over and took the voucher back from Jessie's hand before tearing it slowly into four identically sized pieces.

Jessie could think of nothing else to say even though

she knew that her silence exposed her as being guilty. She walked out of the shop feeling very hot under the collar of her cardigan. Any triumph that she had briefly felt from getting into Stein's office and finding a folder about "Nine Lives" and an identity for "MM" had long since vanished.

Afterwards the boys excitedly told Jessie their side of the story of Jock kicking up a fuss in the shop and Stein's reaction when he appeared behind the counter.

"If he'd snarled any more loudly some of his fish would have flapped on to the floor!" chortled Murdo.

"Even Beanface and Beetroot looked scared," said Fergus, grinning with the memory of the thrill of causing a stir.

"Then he virtually threw us out of the shop and tried to give Jock a kick," said Murdo suddenly going serious.

"Mind you, Jock did try and bite his ankle," said Fergus.

But none of the boys' enthusiasm could lift Jessie out of her downbeat mood and they realized that she felt she had let the side down badly. They tried to cheer her up even though they weren't quite sure how much they had lost or gained from her visit to the shop.

"Jessie, you did well," said Fergus trying to be positive. "We were going nowhere with 'MM2' before today. We can order the book that you saw and see if that helps fit her into the jigsaw. You never know where that might lead."

"And a folder for 'Nine Lives.' That means that we know Stein has a big interest in cat food. That has to be a major breakthrough," added Murdo

"And you saw the microphone," continued Fergus. "That confirms that Stein's property is below the manhole cover."

"But Stein had no idea that anyone was interested in him until today and I don't trust him at all. I think he could be dangerous," said Jessie limping around her living room and unable to settle. "I gave the game away — choosing a stupid surname, mentioning that photo and then this wretched cardigan. I'm just a stupid old woman and I've let you down."

Try as they might the boys found it impossible to reason with Jessie and cheer her up, so they left, agreeing that they would be in touch in the next few days with any developments.

It was Sunday morning when Fergus woke earlier than usual with the sun streaming through his curtains. It had turned into a summer of blue-sky days. He got up and went to the kitchen, pouring himself some cereal while still only half awake. Yawning and bleary-eyed he went to the fridge to find that there was no milk. As he weighed up whether he would be able to swallow dry cereal there was a call from his mum's bedroom.

"Fergus, I forgot to get milk yesterday."

"I was hoping that you'd just decided to hide it somewhere new," said Fergus.

"Be a love and nip out and get some would you? There's some change on the hall table."

"What's in it for me?" called Fergus.

"Cornflakes," said his mum as the noise of a hairdryer started.

The wind blew into Fergus's sleepy eyes as he free-wheeled down Comely Bank Avenue on his bike. He began to wonder how far up the long slow hill he would manage on his way back home. His record was to number 67, but he didn't feel like setting a new personal best today.

The streets were slowly coming to life as Fergus pedalled towards Raeburn Place. Some early birds were heading home from the few shops that were open, clutching pints of milk or reading the newspaper headlines as they walked. Fergus was almost past

Stein's when a sideways glance at the fish shop made him swerve, hit the kerb heavily, veer wildly into the middle of the road and just manage to steady himself again. A man reading his paper as he walked along the pavement looked up in surprise at the sight of a boy out of control on his bike for no apparent reason. Fergus was oblivious to the fact that he had nearly crashed. The only thing occupying his mind as he U-turned and cycled back was what he thought he had just seen in the window of Stein's Fish Shop. He braked sharply outside the shop and saw immediately that, although he had been half-asleep as he cycled past, he certainly hadn't been dreaming. There behind the window on the marble shelf, which was covered with fish during the day but had been washed down for the night, sat ... a cat!

10. Welcome Back, Buster!

Fergus approached the window cautiously feeling as though the cat might vanish if he wasn't careful enough. The cat reacted as soon as it saw him and he could just hear its "meows" through the glass. He put his hand to the window almost expecting to be able to touch it. The cat rubbed up to the glass as if wanting to be stroked. Fergus wondered if it had been a long time since it had been petted. Could this be one of the missing cats sitting in the middle of their prime suspect's shop?

"Don't worry," said Fergus, with both his hands and face now pressed to the glass. "I'll get you out."

He looked around but there was no way in. The shop was well and truly closed until the start of business the next day. Fergus rattled the glass door just to make sure. The cat jumped on to the floor as if in anticipation of being freed.

"I'm sorry. It's locked," said Fergus through the door, as if the cat would understand him.

Fergus looked to the end of the row of shops and remembered the archway from where they'd seen Beanface come and go in his white van.

"I'm going round the back," he said to the cat. The cat looked blankly back and meowed.

Leaving his bike propped up against the shop window Fergus sprinted past a few shops, under the archway and round the corner to the back of the shop. He found it was even more secure than the front. There were bars on the only window, which had frosted glass, and there was a solid door with three padlocks and a firmly-closed metal shutter, giving absolutely no opportunity for rescuing cats.

"What can I do, what can I do?" muttered Fergus, his mind working overtime as he returned to the shop window where the cat still sat waiting for something to happen. Suddenly Fergus knew what he had to do.

"I'm going to get help," he said through the window to the cat, and with that he sped off on his bike. A few minutes before he had only been semi-conscious as he cycled through the early morning streets. Now he was fully awake and his legs were pumping like pistons to get him to Murdo's as quickly as possible.

Fergus made it to Orchard Brae Gardens in record time and hammered on the caravan door. There was silence so he tried again. And again.

"Oi! Dr. Watson! What do you think you're doing?"

Fergus spun around, confused by the location of the voice.

"Up here, Investigator Boy!" said the voice. "You won't solve many cases if you can't even work out where I am."

Fergus looked up to find Heather leaning out of her bedroom window.

"What are you doing waking us all up at this time on a Sunday morning? Big breakthrough in the case is it?"

Fergus smiled and mumbled a bit, desperate to speak to Murdo and not to his sister about what had just happened.

"Yeah something important has come up," he said vaguely. "I need to let your brother know."

"Send Sherlock my love, but keep the noise down while you're doing it," said Heather, closing the window with a thud.

"Go away," groaned Murdo, "it's too early," as Fergus thumped on the caravan door again. Fergus could hear Jock growling sleepily too.

"Get up, you lazy lump," said Fergus urgently, "This is important. This is ... this is ... this is *it!*" he shouted. There was a loud crash and Fergus heard "Ouch ouch ooya ooya ooya," followed by a muffled string of words. The caravan door flew open. Murdo, wild-eyed and even wilder-haired, was clutching the toes on one foot. Despite his dishevelled state he looked as though he had come to his senses almost as quickly as Fergus had when passing the fish shop a few minutes earlier. Jock bounced up and down beside and around Murdo trying to lick his sore foot.

"Come in, come in ... what is it? What *is* it?" asked Murdo glancing out of the caravan into the bright sunlight to check that Fergus wasn't being followed.

"Get the file — the file of all the cats!" said Fergus bursting to tell Murdo what had just happened. "Find a large ginger and white tom, with one white paw and three ginger ones and half of its left ear missing."

"I see your powers of observation are not deserting you," muttered Murdo as he rifled for the folder in his rucksack and began leafing through it, scanning each page systematically to match Fergus's description.

"So where did you see this cat?" asked Murdo, concentrating on the pages as he turned them.

"In the window of Stein's Fish Shop," said Fergus.

Murdo stopped as if he had been switched off. He stared, his jaw sagging in disbelief at Fergus and the folder slipped out of his hands. Anticipating Murdo's next words, Fergus took command. "Yes it's true ... and yes, I'm serious ... before you ask any of those questions ... just check the folder! We've got to track it down and find the owner and get them to the shop before that cat disappears again!"

Murdo shook his head violently as if to clear it and re-focus. He grabbed the folder back off the floor and quickly regained his composure. "Black and white ... tabby ... Persian ..." he muttered, dismissing the descriptions of each cat as they failed to match the one that Fergus had seen in the window.

"Please be there, please be there, please be there," Fergus said quietly under his breath. He was just beginning to realize that there was a chance it was a cat whose owner hadn't even declared it missing, or that there could be some other explanation altogether for a cat being in a fish shop window on a Sunday morning.

"Buster!" said Murdo, as his page turning came to a sudden stop. "Buster is a ginger and white tom, a large cat with one white paw and three ginger ones and half of its left ear missing. Welcome back, Buster!"

"Who are you phoning at this time on a Sunday morning?" asked Mrs. Fraser firmly, as the excited boys huddled over the phone in the house a few minutes later. Fortunately for Murdo his call was answered just before he had to launch into an explanation to his suspicious mother.

"Is that Mrs. Peacock? Hi there ... sorry to call so early ... it's Murdo Fraser here. You may not remember me but I interviewed you a few weeks ago. June 14 to be precise. It was about Buster your missing cat. Well, I think we might have found him. Could you meet me at Stein's Fish Shop at 11am on Raeburn Place? I'll explain when I see you ... yeah, it's good news, he seems to be okay," said Murdo looking at Fergus who nodded.

"So, all your work is finally paying off, is it?" said Mrs. Fraser as Murdo hung up.

"It's a pivotal moment in the case, Mother," said Murdo. "Right, it's your turn," he said handing the phone to Fergus and scrolling through the functions on his DataBoy to retrieve the number that they needed next.

"It's the only way that we might get access to the shop," said Murdo brusquely. "Come on! You spoke to her for longer than I did."

Fergus looked cautiously at Murdo, very nervous about what his friend wanted him to do next. It wasn't really his style. He felt like he was taking his life in his hands, but with a deep breath he dialled the number they'd been given ten days before.

"Can I speak to PC Hall, please?"

There was a long pause, which gave Fergus time to get even more nervous.

"Good morning, PC Hall speaking," said a woman's voice.

"Er ... hallo. It's Fergus Speight here. I don't know if you'll remember me ..."

"Fergus Speight? Oh, Fergus! Hi there. You're not calling from the top of a wall, I hope?"

Fergus went pink and smiled, "No. But do you remember that we were looking for a cat? Well we've found another one that was missing. But it's stuck inside a locked shop."

"Sounds like an unusual start to my Sunday morning shift. Tell me what's been happening and I'll see if I can help," said Gill.

Fergus left the details and Gill promised to do what she could to help. He left a hurried message on Jessie's answermachine to let her know the latest development. The boys then cycled as fast as they could, first to Mrs. Speight's to give her an excited explanation of their plans for Sunday morning, then downhill to the fish shop for their appointment with Mrs. Peacock. Jock's little legs scampered faster than they had ever done before in his efforts to keep up. The boys powered along with the wind whistling in their ears, full of excitement and anticipation that this might be the breakthrough that they needed.

It wasn't long before they came firmly back down to earth. The fish shop looked exactly like most closed fish shops would: locked, spotlessly clean and feline-free.

With no sign of any cat Fergus began to feel the heat rise in prickles at the back of his neck. Murdo glanced over at him but didn't say anything. "It was there," Fergus said firmly. Murdo nodded quietly showing belief and disappointment at the same time.

"We've got company," said Murdo. A police car was pulling up with the familiar face of Gill behind the wheel.

"From both directions," said Fergus looking the other way and watching a large estate car approaching. The woman behind the wheel and a girl about the same age as the boys were both peering out and pointing as they slowed to a halt.

"Hallo again, boys," said Gill. "We must stop meeting like this. So where's this cat then?"

"I saw it in the shop window," said Fergus.

Gill looked at the empty shop window. "Have you been imagining things, Fergus? I hope not because I've managed to get someone to come out and open up the shop, although he didn't sound too happy about it."

The woman from the estate car joined them on the pavement. "Is it true? Have you really found Buster?" The introductions were made with Mrs. Peacock and her daughter, Gemma, while Murdo opened the file on Buster, and Fergus confirmed the description of the cat he had seen, much to the delight of its owners.

"We've got more company," said Murdo nodding towards an approaching white van with the unmistakable figure of Beanface at the wheel.

"Oh no," groaned Fergus. "I'm beginning to have a bad feeling about this."

The white van pulled up and Beanface slid out of the driver's seat, his face so scrunched up with displeasure that he looked like he had just taken a huge bite out of a giant lemon.

"I don't have keys for the front," he grumbled to the small crowd gathered in front of the shop. The motley crew followed him through the archway to the courtyard at the back, stopping at the heavily secured back doors that Fergus had been outside an hour before. The security measures at the fish shop even forced a comment from Gill.

"That must be some fish that you have stored in there," she said lightly.

"You can never be too careful these days," snapped Beanface unlocking the first in a series of padlocks on the door. "You never know who might want to try and get in for a look around," he said with a sideways glance at the boys.

"Or what might be trying to get out," said Murdo feeling aggrieved.

Gill shot him a warning glance as if to say, "That'll do, Murdo."

With a click and a clunk the third padlock was removed and Beanface heaved open the heavy back door. There was silence.

"Well, what did you expect?" said Beanface turning to face them with a crooked smile.

There was a long pause, as the Peacocks looked disappointed, Gill looked annoyed and Fergus and Murdo looked crestfallen.

It was then that a cat shot out of the open door, between Beanface's legs.

"BUSTER!" squealed Gemma in delight as Jock barked and promptly gave chase to the speeding cat.

It was the next day before they had a chance to see Jessie, as she had been away for a few days. The boys laughed when they told Jessie of Beanface's shocked expression when the cat ran out between his legs.

"It nearly tripped him up," said Fergus laughing through a mouthful of warm jammy pancake.

"He would have deserved that and more," said Jessie feeling significantly more upbeat than the last time the boys had seen her. "What did your policewoman friend say?"

"Gill just grinned and said 'Well done,'" said Fergus. "There wasn't a lot more she could do, I suppose. Beanface said that the cat must have sneaked in there during the day some time, so it wasn't like she could search the place for more cats."

"... and the Peacocks didn't seem too interested in how the cat had got there. They were just relieved to have their cat back and we're going to get a £30 reward!" said Murdo.

"Are you going to put it in the kitty?" asked Jessie.

"Ha, ha, very witty," said Fergus.

At that moment the doorbell rang and Jessie disappeared for a minute. She arrived back in the room clutching a package. "I think this is my order from the bookshop," she said starting to tear into the padded envelope.

"Is it *Karate for OAPs*?" asked Murdo mischievously.

Jessie let his comment pass as she held the book in front of her.

"Well, well, well. What do we have here? Our 'MM' appears to be rather highly qualified. She's *Doctor* Maxine McDermott," said Jessie, peering over her glasses and reading the cover. She held the book up so that the boys could see it. "I decided to see where her interests lay, in case it helped us at all so I ordered this the other day."

"Is it a medical book?" asked Murdo.

"Mmm ... not really," said Jessie reading off the inside cover. "*Total Recall* looks at the areas of the brain relating to memory and reports on new technology that can identify individual cells that contain information relating to particular functions."

Flicking through the book, it soon became clear that it would take some time to find out just what "MM" had written about and what practical use any of her ideas had for fish shops. The only page that the three of them tried to make sense of, without success, was one of very few pictures in the book, which showed a machine called the Recall Processor. It looked like a dentist's chair with a helmet and a set of headphones attached to it.

"I suggest that I become our official researcher," said Jessie. "I'll take a day or two to plough through this and I'll get in touch once I've got something useful from it."

"Once you do? More like *if* you do," said Murdo, not holding out much hope of it being a productive lead.

"What have you got planned for today, Fergus?" asked Mrs. Speight over breakfast the next morning.

Fergus shrugged as he put some buttery toast into his mouth. "Might catch up with Murdo," he said, just as the phone rang.

"You get it," said Mrs. Speight. "You're more popular than me these days."

"You'd better come," Murdo's voice said mournfully over the phone.

"What's wrong?" said Fergus.

"Just come."

Minutes later Fergus cycled round the corner into Murdo's street to find a police car parked outside the Frasers' house.

As Fergus wheeled his bike into the drive he found Mrs. Fraser standing over Murdo who was sitting on the front step of the house, his head propped gloomily in his hands.

"Well, there will be no more nights for you in there, young man," said Mrs. Fraser. "You could have been murdered in your bed! What about Fergus?" she said, seeming to know he'd arrived without even seeing him. "How would I have explained that to his mother?"

Fergus looked at the Incident Room. The door to the caravan was swinging open and the window closest to it was broken. A curtain was fluttering pathetically like a surrender flag behind the smashed pane. From where he stood it looked as though every single piece of paper was scattered around inside. The books were off the shelf and the drawers in the filing cabinet were all open and ransacked. Any filing system that Murdo had ever spent hours inventing was long gone. A policewoman stepped out of the caravan.

"We'll have to stop meeting like this," she said brightly looking at the boys. Mrs. Fraser threw a hard and searching stare at Murdo. It was Gill.

"Was that all of your work in there? I see now why you were so interested in tracking cats. You've certainly been busy."

She turned to Mrs. Fraser. "I'm sorry you've had all of this inconvenience. I'm afraid to say that there are occasional break-ins like this in the area. It's usually just a random person looking for money. They make a terrible mess, trying every nook and cranny.

"Unless, that is, you think that there's a rival looking for the cats," she said turning to the boys and trying to inject some humour into the situation.

Fergus toyed with the idea of telling her everything that they had worked on to date.

"Well, what if someone was on to us?" said Fergus. Murdo shot him a glance as if to say he wanted to keep their work a secret, but then looked like he couldn't really be bothered.

"Who would be 'on to you'?" asked Gill.

"The people who have the cats," said Fergus beginning to think that this was not going to be a helpful conversation. "Stein's Fish Shop."

"Why do you think that the fish shop is behind all these cats going missing?" said Gill.

"Well, they own lots of vaults and the guy who owns the shop knows a bit about cats, he did a research thing on what they like to eat and I think he has an interest in a new type of cat food and they have a guy who you never see who has a laptop ..."

"And ...?" said Gill.

Suddenly Fergus realized that the story was beginning to sound a bit thin. Surely they had produced a stronger case than this when they had all thought it through before.

"Buster was in there yesterday," said Fergus playing his last card and knowing that it wasn't enough.

"Sorry, Fergus, that won't stand up in court," said Gill. Fergus couldn't quite believe that their evidence suddenly sounded so unconvincing because he was so sure that they had the right answer. He went over the facts again and again in his mind as he helped to get the Incident Room tidied up.

Murdo of course knew where everything should be and he directed Fergus precisely as they returned things to their rightful place. It was only as they got the last books onto shelves and papers into drawers that it dawned on Murdo what was missing.

"The file of cats and the Investigation Diary," he said, looking crestfallen.

"What about them?" asked Fergus.

"They're gone," he said.

"Never mind," said Fergus trying desperately to be positive. "We've entered everything on the database so we still have all of the information on every cat."

Murdo perked up momentarily but then his shoulders slumped again. "But the diary ... if they have that it means that they know everything that we know. They know exactly where we are in our investigation."

Fergus couldn't think of anything encouraging to say at that point because he had to admit that it did all seem a bit bleak. It was as if they had shown every card in their hand to their opponent.

That evening the boys managed to negotiate for Fergus to stay over, although this time it was on a Z-bed in Murdo's bedroom. Mrs. Fraser had insisted on calling Fergus's mum to explain what had happened with the caravan. The boys couldn't understand why she felt she had to apologize for this and they shuffled about feeling awkward as they listened in to one side of the conversation.

The eventful day finished on a much brighter note, and memories of the break-in began to fade as Mrs. Peacock appeared during the evening with the reward money promised for the successful outcome with Buster.

"Just dropping off your £30," she said cheerily, "and to take the opportunity to say 'thanks' again. You've made Gemma's year."

"How is your cat?" asked Mrs. Fraser.

"Buster seems fine," said Mrs. Peacock. "He just seems to be off his food but the vet said it shouldn't be anything to worry about."

Fergus and Murdo looked at each other and raised their eyebrows. Was it just a coincidence that a cat that had spent at least some time in Stein's Fish Shop should have lost its appetite?

11. The Five Senses

The next morning, the doorbell rang and from the kitchen Fergus could make out his mum talking to someone else on the doorstep before asking them in.

"Hi, Fergus." It was Narveen.

"Do you need a cat sitter again?" asked Fergus wondering if he trusted Sasha not to lead him into trouble again.

"Sasha has gone missing, Fergus," said Narveen. "I've just come round to see if you'd seen her recently."

"No ... I'm sorry," said Fergus, stunned to hear that a cat had gone missing so close to home. "When did you last see her?"

"The night before last, but then she wasn't around yesterday and she's not back this morning. It's just not like her. I know she's independent but she's never been away this long before."

"Hmmm," said Fergus remembering just how independent Sasha had been when they were trying to keep up with her.

"We'll certainly keep an eye open for you," said Fergus's mum. "Fergus found someone else's cat the other day. In fact he was escorted back to the house by a policewoman. Very nice she was too, but I suspect the neighbours will be thinking I have a delinquent son. They could be right, of course."

Fergus stuck his tongue out at his mum.

"See what I mean?" said his mum with a smile.

"Did anything unusual happen around the time she went missing?" asked Fergus, thinking through some of the questions that he knew Murdo would want to ask.

123

"No, I got back from work late-ish. Had trouble parking. It was even worse than usual, because there was one space right outside but it was blocked by a white van that was double-parked. The guy was just sitting behind the wheel and he was quite rude when I asked him to move."

"What did he look like?" asked Fergus, his interest rising.

He could almost predict Narveen's answer. "Sort of skinny with a sharp nose," she said.

Gill's words, "That wouldn't stand up in court," rang in Fergus's head.

"Oh, yes it would," he thought as he pictured Narveen trying to get Beanface to move his white van. As she left their flat Fergus told her that he and Murdo would add Sasha's details to the list of lost cats. It seemed that no sooner had they found one cat in the shape of Buster, than another went missing. The running total remained at forty-four.

In order to be thorough before reporting back to Murdo, Fergus decided to look out into the road where the double-parking incident had taken place. As he went to the edge of the pavement, he disturbed a scraggy seagull, which flew up from the road with a squawk. Comely Bank Avenue was quiet and Fergus went between the parked cars to look at where it had been pecking between the cobblestones. There on the road were a few scraps of what looked like flakes of fish.

"That must have been a high tide," thought Fergus. "How did they get there?"

Fergus decided that Murdo and Jessie should hear about Sasha's disappearance, Beanface's double-parking and the fact that fish had landed on Comely Bank Avenue.

"Boys, this shows us that there is an important missing link," said Jessie later, "and I've got some more interesting developments to add. We believe that the cats are in the shop, although if we try any harder to prove that they're on the premises we're going to get ourselves in big trouble. Now I've been running a few queries on all of the data that you entered ... look."

Jessie handed Fergus and Murdo a printout with lots of figures on. "Did you know that all of the cats from the same streets disappeared on the same day? It's like they are being gathered together somehow. It's time we concentrated on how we think the cats are getting *to* the shop. The way I see it is that there can only be two options ..."

Jumping up, Murdo interrupted. "The cats all go there because there's a high pitched noise that only cats can hear that the white van plays and all the cats follow the van like something out of the Pied Piper, only it's cats not rats and they end up in the vaults and ..."

"Sorry, Murdo," said Jessie, "I might almost have believed you this time, except that no one has reported seeing long lines of cats following a white van through the streets of Comely Bank. That might just be a bit obvious. I think the two options are that either the cats are *somehow* all making their way to the shop of their own accord or else they are being taken there forcibly."

"I think there's another option," said Fergus. "What if they are quite happy to be taken there?"

"Mmm ... interesting thought, Fergus," Jessie nodded, "But surely, however it's happening, we would see a lot of coming and going from the shop."

"Well, the main thing coming and going is Beanface in his white van," said Murdo flicking through his stakeout notebook. "Beanface came and went from the shop in the van an average of 7.3 times a day."

"And that's just during the day. Who knows what he's up to at night?" added Fergus.

"It's certainly suspicious that he was around when Sasha was last seen," said Jessie, "and the fish on the road is almost like the leftovers of some bait that was put out to attract cats. I think that we need to find a way of checking the white van and finding out what our friend, Beanface, gets up to when he's out and about."

"How do we get a look at the van?" said Murdo.

"I don't want any more late-night escapades," said Jessie. "Ideally, we would want to look at it in broad daylight without anyone getting suspicious."

"It needs to be away from the shop then," said Fergus.

"Right here, in fact, if we could just distract Beanface for a while," said Murdo.

"It can't be us — he'd be very suspicious if we were involved. We need something where he gets held up for ages even though he thought he'd only be a few seconds," said Jessie.

"Sounds like Beryl Scrimgeour," joked Fergus. "Talking to her always means that you're there longer than you planned."

"That's it!" Jessie exclaimed. "Beryl would be brilliant for this!"

It took Jessie a long time to explain to Beryl Scrimgeour why she had a part to play in the next stage of the investigation, but then that proved the point that any time spent with her was always a long time. When Jessie finally got back to the flat, after speaking to Mrs. Scrimgeour about her idea for a simple way to repay her for hanging her mirror, she told the boys that she was "One hundred per cent confident" that Mrs. Scrimgeour could play her part to the full.

The next plan that came out of Jessie's dusty living room was that Beryl would order some fish from Stein's by phone and ask to have it delivered. The success of the operation then hinged on three key factors. Firstly, that Beanface's white van would appear for the delivery. Secondly, that Beanface would leave the van open thinking that he was dropping something off in a few seconds, and thirdly, that Beryl Scrimgeour could occupy him for at least fifteen minutes inside her flat. There was little doubt about the last of these, so the first two would be left to chance.

It was agreed that while Beanface was occupied, the boys would have as good a look as they could around the van, and for once, one of Murdo's suggestions was actually quite a good one.

"Why don't we play with a ball on the pavement and 'accidentally' lose it under the van in order to get a closer look?" His round face lit up as Jessie and Fergus agreed that this would give the boys more of a reason for being near the van.

The plan was set for the following morning, shortly before Jessie was due to be picked up for a long-standing two-day trip away. With her bags packed and standing in the hall, she and the boys positioned themselves in her front room with a plate of date and walnut muffins, ready for the action to begin. The boys had the same sense of excitement as the time they had headed out at night to try to look under the manhole cover. Jessie managed to persuade Murdo that he did not need a full rucksack of equipment in order to look at the van. He insisted that there were a few items that "just might come in useful" and had negotiated her down to a couple of bulging trouser pockets of paper clips, bits of string and assorted tools.

Jessie had once again given the boys her old mobile phone. This time Fergus had it attached to his belt with an earpiece in his ear. He found that the earpiece didn't stay in very well, so Jessie and Murdo had enjoyed taping it to his ear. Fergus was not looking forward to taking it off at the end of the operation.

Jessie meanwhile was equipped with a large pair of ancient-looking binoculars from a brown leather case, which had belonged to Stan. "He'd be shocked if he thought I was using them to watch the neighbours," said Jessie. "I've heard of curtain-twitching old ladies, but this is ridiculous," she added, focusing the binoculars on Beryl's flat. Finally the boys synchronized their DataBoys and both prepared their stopwatches and alarms for a period of fifteen minutes.

As they waited, Jessie remembered to tell the boys about her progress with her research. "I must admit I've struggled a bit with that book and I do wonder if Stein has it on his bookshelves just because MM is his girlfriend. Her research is all about which bits of the brain do which things and she's invented some scanner that shows where memory cells are in the brain. I can't really see the connection with cats or fish shops. In fact it all seems like a bit of a red herring to me, if you'll excuse the joke."

"Well, the van is a good new line of enquiry," said Murdo, "so let's put our resources in that direction."

They didn't have to wait long as shortly after eleven o'clock the familiar white van pulled up outside Beryl's flat.

"That's it now," said Jessie, the binoculars fixed firmly to her face. "It's Beanface," she confirmed as the lanky man hopped out of the van. "And he's not locked it," she said triumphantly as she watched him kick the driver's door shut and head for Beryl's front door carrying a low-sided box. "He's ringing the bell. Okay, boys ... on your marks ..." said Jessie.

As if a blue light had been switched on, Beryl Scrimgeour appeared at the door and welcomed Beanface like a long lost son. Before he could say "forty-four cats" he seemed to have been sucked inside, and as Beryl closed the door she gave a deep nod which she knew would be seen by Jessie.

"Right boys, off to work." said Jessie. "You've got fifteen minutes. And remember when I say 'time up,' I mean 'time up.'"

The boys hit the stopwatches on their DataBoys and

sped out of Jessie's flat with Jock hot on their heels. They crossed the road bouncing the ball as they went. As they approached the van, Murdo let go of the ball, letting it roll towards the van and under the back bumper.

"Good shot," said Fergus as the ball disappeared. He bent down to see where it had got to and found that he would have to lie down and stretch an arm or a leg under in order to get it out. Murdo meanwhile went to the driver's door and peered in before cautiously opening it and climbing in with Jock nosing in behind him. Fergus tried to reach under the van with his leg to get the ball but found that he couldn't quite stretch far enough.

"Is the handbrake on?" said Fergus.

"Yep it's on," said Murdo.

"Here goes!" he thought to himself as he went headfirst and began to crawl under the van. He hadn't got very far when there was an excited shout from Murdo.

"I can see you!"

"What?" said Fergus seeing no sign of his friend.

"There's a screen here and there must be wee cameras close to where you are!" Murdo's voice bellowed.

"Keep your voice down a bit!" hissed Fergus spotting the tiny eye of a camera lens about two feet from his head.

"WHAT? SPEAK UP I CAN'T HEAR YOU!" shouted Murdo even louder.

"SSSSHHHHHH!" said Fergus.

"Oh, yeah, right enough, sorry."

"Cameras under a van that delivers fish. Very strange," thought Fergus although there was now little that would surprise him about Stein's Fish Shop.

Buzzzzzz whirrrrrr.

Fergus edged his head around trying to locate the low purring mechanical sound.

A large flat metal plate on four rods like an upside-down table with extending telescopic legs was descending from the floor of the van and came to rest on the road beside where he lay.

"What did you do?" asked Fergus.

"Pressed a button," said Murdo.

"Which one?"

"It's called 'Capture Plate,'" said Murdo.

Fergus thought for a moment, "So why would a cat step on to this?"

Sensing that they were near to an important discovery, he called out to Murdo, "Press some more buttons!"

A low soothing voice said "puss puss ... puss puss," close to his right ear. He eased his head round to find a tiny speaker on the underside of the van. "What was that button?"

"'Sound,'" said Murdo.

"Try another," said Fergus. Seconds later with another low whirring noise, two panels descended from the underside of the van. They began to move in like bookends coming together and stopped to form walls along the side of the Capture Plate. Fergus noticed that the panels were vibrating slightly and as he tentatively put his hand out to touch them he found that this caused a ticklish sensation.

"Touch — another sense," said Fergus to himself.

"Are there another three buttons?" asked Fergus beginning to realize why the van was so appealing to cats.

"Yes. How did you know?" said Murdo. "I'll try them all," he continued just as Fergus shouted, "Don't press any more!"

"Yikes!" yelped Fergus as a mouse landed on the road right beside his head and disappeared again. Suddenly it was there again and he realized that it was a very effective imitation mouse on some very thin wire, released and then recaptured like the bird from a cuckoo clock from a tiny box on the underside of the van.

"Yeeuk!" cried Fergus as he got a faceful of fish odours blown out from a small vent above him.

Whoosh splat!

"Eeurgh!" choked Fergus as he was hit in the face by a spray of soggy fish flakes fired from a small dispensing pipe near to his head.

"That'll be sight, smell and taste then," he said pulling his hand around in the tight confines to wipe his face. "No cat could resist something that appealed to each of its senses. Beanface has every option covered."

Unperturbed by the onslaught, Fergus went for a closer look at the hole in the van's floor that had appeared when the Capture Plate was lowered. By crawling on to the plate and squeezing his body upwards Fergus was able to get himself through the narrow gap and into the van — something that anyone of Murdo's size could only have dreamt about.

As he poked his head through the floor and into the inside of the van, Fergus silently apologized to his friend as he realized that sometimes even his wilder ideas might just have the possibility of being true.

"I can see you, I can see you," said Murdo's now muffled but clearly excited voice through the van wall. Fergus could certainly see why Murdo could see him. There were tiny cameras in every corner of the van. Most of the inside was taken up by rectangular cages which were stacked five high against the walls. At a quick guess Fergus reckoned there were about fifty cages in total.

Along the edge of the cages ran a small conveyor belt and there was a hoist which sat in one corner like a tiny crane. Fergus could see that the cages could be moved around the back of the van on the conveyor belts to fit over the Capture Plate. This meant that from the driver's seat Beanface had complete control not just of driving the van but of what went on in the back of it too. He could tour the streets, attracting cats to come under the van by appealing to each of their senses. A quick press of the right buttons and any cat would be captured by the closing walls on the side of the plate, lifted up and caged in the van in a matter of seconds.

The fish shop van was a one-man cat-capturing machine.

"This is amazing. Anything else of interest where you are?" called Fergus. Murdo's voice came back through the van wall. "Not really, although there is a number on a bit of paper stuck to the dashboard that might be useful. If you'd let me bring my notebook and pen I could have written it down. Can you remember it? You're better than me at those things. It says 'Access Code: 51329.'"

"I'll use my watch," said Fergus, keying the number into the memory of his DataBoy. Fergus had just finished when the phone rang loudly in his earpiece.

"Boys, your time is nearly up, I want you to get out in the next sixty seconds," Jessie's voice crackled.

"Jessie says time up and no buts, Murdo."

"But ..." began Murdo before realizing that Jessie had anticipated his reaction.

"I'll go back the way I came in," said Fergus through the wall to Murdo, "then you'd better raise the Capture Plate again and leave everything as you found it."

Fergus squeezed himself through the gap in the floor of the van as quickly as he could, edging his way onto the Capture Plate and back to the road. As he crawled out from under the van, the mechanism for the Capture Plate began to buzz and whirr again and the device disappeared back into the underside of the van. Fergus hooked his left foot around the football which was still wedged waiting to be rescued. Anyone who had been watching might well have wondered why it had taken a boy fifteen minutes to get his ball out from under a van.

As Fergus brushed himself down, Murdo hopped out of the van, closing the door behind him. The alarms on the two DataBoys went off in unison.

"Time up! A perfectly executed operation!" said Murdo looking at his watch and grinning from ear to ear.

Fergus waved the ball. "Game of football, Murdo?"

"Don't mind if I do, Fergus!" replied Murdo.

"Let's just see if Jessie wants a game first," said Fergus trotting back across the road to Jessie's flat.

Over the next few minutes they recounted the tale of the successful operation to Jessie who remained in position at the window to keep an eye on the last stage of events. Murdo described the findings at the van as "cast-iron evidence" that linked the fish shop to the cats' disappearance. Fergus meanwhile kept rubbing at his face which he was convinced stank of fish.

Jessie interrupted them, as Beanface finally emerged from Beryl's front door looking distinctly hot and bothered. The boys crowded in to peer through the net curtains with her. According to Murdo's DataBoy, he had been in there for twenty-three minutes and forty seconds and his face was almost the colour of his colleague Beetroot's. Beryl gave a heavy wink in the direction of Jessie's flat as she waved him off. Beanface accelerated away angrily, the white van roaring off down Comely Bank Avenue.

As they speculated on just how many cats might have been captured in the van over the last few months and taken to the fish shop, Fergus realized that Murdo had drifted out of the conversation. In fact he was sitting very quiet and was somehow looking smaller, almost as though he had shrunk in on himself. He had also gone very pale.

"Murdo, are you feeling all right?" asked Fergus.

"Er, I don't think this operation has been quite the success that we thought," said Murdo.

"What is it? What's wrong?" said Jessie.

"Did we miss something?" asked Fergus.

"I left something important in the van," said Murdo.

Fergus looked expectantly at Murdo and waited to hear him mention a piece of equipment. He was certainly not expecting what Murdo said next.

"Jock."

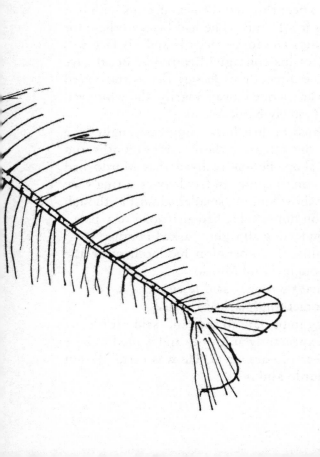

12. The Rescue Attempt

"He must have fallen asleep. He just curled up on the passenger side when we climbed in. When the call came to get out I completely forgot that he was there." It was Murdo's turn to pace the room looking utterly perplexed. His arms were one wave and a clutch away from tearing his hair out.

Fergus swallowed hard. It wouldn't have taken Beanface long to realize that there was a dog in the van and even less time to make a connection with the recent dog incident in the shop. It seemed that each time they found out more about Stein's shop they gave something else away about themselves.

Jessie looked equally concerned. "I feel that this takes us into new territory. We certainly mustn't do anything rash. I think that it may be time to call your friend Gill again. After all we need to tell her about that van and what it's being used for."

"I've got to go and find him," said Murdo completely caught up in his own world. "It won't do any harm just to have a look around down at the shop. He might be wandering about looking a bit lost. I mean maybe he hid from Beanface and he's escaped. He's very resourceful you know."

Fergus smiled weakly. Smart though Jock was, it seemed more likely that he would have started some frenzied barking rather than made a cunning decision to hide when Beanface got back into the van.

"I'll call Gill," said Fergus feeling a bit more confident about using his contact now and keen to do anything to help Murdo calm down. The message he got a minute or two later however put the dampers back on the day.

"She's not at work for another three hours," he said glumly as he put the phone down.

"Boys, I think you should sit tight until then. She is the main person that could help to negotiate with this one. You can call her in a few hours and tell her all about the van and get her to help with Jock. Now I'm going to have to get ready. I'll be heading off soon as my lift arrives in about half an hour. You keep that mobile phone for now, Fergus, and listen to me carefully ..."

The two boys sat on the settee looking up expectantly at Jessie. She leaned forward in her armchair and looked at them firmly. "You boys must *not* do anything until you get hold of Gill. We don't know for sure what Stein is up to, but I know he's someone not to be trifled with. Do you hear me? You need to promise me you won't go marching off and start something that you can't predict the finish of."

"Yes," mumbled Fergus, conscious that Murdo seemed to be looking in a different direction, intent on not taking part in this conversation and certainly avoiding promising Jessie anything.

A few minutes later Jessie showed them out of her flat past two bulging bags in the hall. "Sorry, I'm leaving you to it, but this trip has been booked for a long time," she said. "Now remember what I said."

"Well that's that until later," said Fergus as they headed out on to Comely Bank Avenue. "I'm sure that Jock will be alright for a few hours," he said, trying to convince himself as much as Murdo.

"I can't leave him there with that animal thief! He likes an adventure but that's taking it too far!" cried Murdo. "We have to do something. I'm not waiting around for half a day!"

"Jessie told us not to do anything until later. You heard her.

She thinks it's getting too risky. Don't forget she met Stein. She seems to think he's got a nasty streak."

Fergus's words seemed to go nowhere as Murdo said flatly, "I'm going to the shop, Fergus. You can come if you want to and you can stay if you want to, but I'm going to find Jock."

Murdo began to walk off, his rucksack bobbing on his back as he went.

Faced with the choice of letting Murdo down or going against Jessie's wishes was not a place that Fergus wanted to find himself in. He had heard people talking about "going with their head or their heart." He found that his head was definitely saying "You don't know what you're getting involved in and you can't be sure where it will lead," but his heart was telling him convincingly, "Murdo needs all the help he can get and you can't leave Jock anywhere near a shop where animals have a bad habit of going missing." He ran to catch up with his friend.

After some debate, Fergus managed to convince Murdo that the best plan was to keep it simple. This meant having a look around near the shop to see if the van was there and seeing if there was any immediate sign of Jock. So, with a feeling of trepidation rather than excitement, they headed off once again, as quickly as they could, to the fish shop. Fergus glanced back as they went almost expecting to see Jessie wagging her finger disapprovingly at them.

There was a buzz of shoppers around when they arrived and it seemed to be a normal working day on Raeburn Place with Stein's doing a steady trade.

The boys slipped through the archway and round the lane to the back of the shop. There was no sign of the van or any other vehicle. The metal shutter was down and locked and the only other thing of note was a neat pile of large white plastic boxes stacked up on one side of the courtyard.

"Let's see if that door is locked as tightly as it was on Sunday morning," said Murdo. Before Fergus could caution him about going too close, Murdo was off and running, and seconds later was rattling the door, finding it unsurprisingly shut tight.

As Murdo turned away disappointed, the roar of a rapidly approaching engine began to fill the courtyard. There was a split second as the boys stared at each other wide-eyed before they dived for cover behind the stack of white containers. A second later the boys peeked out to see the familiar white van pulling up to the metal shutter.

"That was close," whispered Fergus.

"Very," said Murdo, large beads of sweat breaking out on his round face. He squeezed out of his rucksack straps and wafted his shirt in an attempt to cool down.

The boys could hear the sound of the van's engine idling and the driver's door being opened and closed. The next noise was the rattle of locks and then the protesting scrape of metal on metal. The boys nodded in silent agreement that the shuttered door had just been rolled back. Then the van engine cut out, there were some footsteps and all became quiet. The boys looked at each other and shrugged. The only sound now was the distant buzz of cars on Raeburn Place.

"Was it Beanface driving?" asked Murdo.

"I suspect so," said Fergus adjusting his crouching position, "although I couldn't see properly. I was too busy going headfirst to get out of the way."

"Why's it so quiet?" said Murdo.

Fergus took a deep breath and peeked around the corner of the stack of white containers. The van had reversed up to the shuttered door which was now open. Everything was still.

"There's no one there and the doors are open." Even as he said it Fergus realized that he had made a mistake in giving such an accurate description.

Murdo's eyes lit up. "Right, I'm going to have a look."

"That's not a good idea," said Fergus firmly. "Beanface would never leave that door open for long. He'll be back any minute."

"It has to be done! It might be our only chance to look for Jock." Murdo was already on his way as he finished the sentence, in such a rush that he left his rucksack lying on the ground.

"Jessie would not be happy with this," was the main thought running through Fergus's mind as he hesitated, then put on the rucksack and followed Murdo towards the open shuttered door. Up ahead Murdo looked through the driver's window into the van but didn't see anything worth breaking his stride for.

"Jock!" he whispered urgently as he tiptoed towards the open shuttered door. "Jock?"

There was no reply. Fergus was now level with Murdo, his heart thumping so fast that it seemed to have moved up to his ears. The boys were just inside what was a gloomy loading bay. As their eyes adjusted to the dim light they could see that there were lots more white containers and not much else of note. Murdo started lifting the lids on a few of the containers as if expecting Jock to suddenly appear from one of them. Fergus couldn't imagine that the little dog was in any of these and looking around the area, he felt that they were also in the wrong part of the building to have any chance of finding him.

He glanced back to the pile of boxes that they had left behind. They suddenly seemed a long long way off. If they needed to dive for cover again, they would have to sprint some distance first and Fergus began to feel very exposed.

As he looked out into the yard there was a flash of colour

to the left of the boxes where they had hidden a moment or two before. It came and went so quickly that if he had blinked he would have missed it but it seemed to him that there was something else out there. He turned to ask Murdo if he had seen anything but suddenly remembered that they were in mid-trespass.

"We should get out," said Fergus. "This isn't the place to look. Beanface will be back any second."

"I'm just going to check the back of the van," said Murdo, giving up on the boxes and paying no attention to Fergus's concern. "You look in some more of these containers."

Fergus shook his head in exasperation as Murdo went off to the van.

"This is not good," Fergus muttered to himself, but he quickly started to look around in the slim hope that Jock was nearby. Everything seemed as a loading bay should be. Brick walls, a concrete floor, lots of containers and certainly no sign of a stray dog. Glancing up he realized that Murdo had disappeared from view. The back door of the van was slightly open and he could just see Murdo through the crack.

Fergus looked back at the containers beside him and a flash of blue amidst the white plastic caught his eye. Looking more closely he reached down and pulled out a plastic clipboard which appeared to have slipped between two of the containers. A single sheet of paper was attached to the metal clasp at the top, and on it was a long list of place names: Dumfries, Dundee, Falkirk, Newcastle, Perth, Stirling. Beside each was a number.

Fergus tried to make sense of the list. "Dundee 35, Falkirk 24?" he mused, distracted from the fact that he was standing somewhere that he shouldn't be. "Well, Dundee supporters would be happy."

Fergus looked up to see if Murdo was anywhere nearby to help him puzzle this one through, when suddenly he froze as he heard a door close. There was the sound of footsteps approaching from the other side of a door at the back of the loading bay that led towards the shop. The hairs on the back of his neck stood up.

"Quick! Someone's coming!" he called towards the van, realizing that whoever was approaching was already only a matter of steps away and was about to appear.

"Murdo, get out now!" said Fergus as loudly as he dared towards the van, sliding the clipboard back between the containers. There was now no time to get out of the loading bay unseen and with seconds to go Fergus dived for one of the white containers which was standing open with its lid to one side. In a flash he was inside it, clumsily falling in because of Murdo's rucksack. He pulled the plastic lid over his head just in time as he heard the door at the back of the loading bay open.

Fergus breathed heavily and tried to control his racing heart pounding in his ears. He didn't know if Murdo had heard his warning but as the footsteps of whoever had just entered the loading bay passed by and headed out to the courtyard, there seemed to be no way that his friend would have got out of the van in time.

Fergus buried his head in his hands. He couldn't believe that the rescue attempt had ended with no clue as to Jock's whereabouts, Murdo caught and him stuck in a plastic box. They had hit a new all time low.

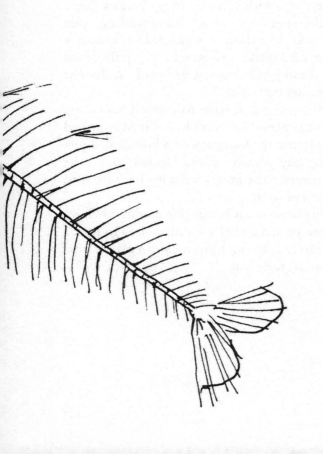

13. Going Underground

Flicking on his DataBoy's tiny light, Fergus saw that it was now two minutes since he had made the snap decision to use the white box as a hiding place. As soon as he had pulled the lid over himself he had been overpowered by the stench of fish and by the realization that he now had no way of knowing what was happening beyond the four white plastic walls of the box. His eyes soon adjusted to the gloom but there was absolutely nothing to see in the smooth-sided container. There weren't even any remnants of whatever had left the strong smell behind but there was no doubt that it had been some sort of fish. Fergus didn't know how long the box had been used to store fish or how many would have been in there, but he reckoned the answer to those questions would be "ages" and "lots." There was a small pool of cold liquid on the floor of the container and he could feel his trousers beginning to get damp, and guessed that he was probably almost as smelly as the container itself.

Still, it had at least proved to be the right place to hide. He had remained undiscovered since the door at the back of the loading bay had opened. Fergus had held his breath as it did so and concentrated on trying not to move a muscle, although this had seemed to be harder to do the more he had thought about it. He had become suddenly aware of an itch above his left ankle, a muscle had started to twitch in his right shoulder and a piece of walnut from one of Jessie's muffins that had lodged between his teeth had begun to annoy him. Fergus had tried to put any idea of scratching, rubbing or poking out of his mind and channelled his thoughts into listening as hard as he could.

The footsteps and rustling were worryingly close to

where he was hiding and Fergus had tried to picture what might be going on outside the box. He imagined that it was Beanface looking around for the clipboard that he had been puzzling over seconds before the door opened.

Soon the rustling had stopped and the footsteps began again but seemed to be heading away from where Fergus lay still, and he imagined Beanface heading towards the van. Having seen inside the van earlier that day Fergus knew that there would be no place for Murdo to hide, so unless he had got out of the van as quickly as Fergus had dived into the box, he would surely be caught. Knowing Murdo's lack of speed, this seemed likely and Fergus began to worry seriously for Murdo's safety.

As if to answer his fears, Fergus heard distant voices; sharp and raised from Beanface, high and protesting from Murdo. He couldn't make out the words initially but he could guess the kind of exchange that was taking place as Beanface discovered an intruder in his van. Confusingly at the same time, he heard a shuffling noise nearby in the loading bay as if something else was nearby. He strained to make sense of the noise but failed. Gradually however, he began to pick up voices coming closer from the direction of the van and soon made out some words.

"Where are you taking me?" he heard Murdo shout. He seemed to be putting a bit of extra volume into his normally loud voice, and Fergus guessed that this was his way of communicating that he had been caught and was now being taken on to the premises.

"Shut up. You'll find out soon enough," said Beanface cutting him off abruptly.

"Where's my dog?" Murdo's shrill voice rang out.

"Safe and sound," said Beanface menacingly, as a metallic rattle signalled that the shutter of the loading bay was being lowered, closing both boys inside the premises, one in a box and one in Beanface's bony clutches.

"If you've harmed him ..." began Murdo.

"You'll do what?" snapped Beanface, as the voices headed away through the door at the back of the loading bay towards the inside of the building. Once again Fergus strained to hear any noise that would give him a clue as to what was happening. The last sound that he could make out as the footsteps disappeared was a single solid "clang," which dissolved into the air like a fading church bell, leaving him in silence.

Fergus sat in the box, beginning to breathe more easily now that he knew he was on his own, although his mind was spinning about what he should do next. One thing became clear to him. It was now up to him to rescue not just Jock the dog, but his owner as well.

Allowing another three minutes to pass on his DataBoy, Fergus reckoned that it was as safe outside the box as it was likely to get. He lifted the lid a fraction and peered out. It was now much darker in the loading bay since Beanface had lowered the metal shutter. Fergus heaved himself stiffly out of the box. All of his mystery itches disappeared as soon as he stood up and began to stretch, but the one thing that didn't change was that he now had a pair of damp and extremely smelly trousers as a souvenir of spending five minutes in the fish container.

Although he could see that he was alone in the loading bay, Fergus kept as still as he could as though the slightest movement might set off some hidden alarm system. Willing his eyes to adjust as quickly as possible to the dim light, he tiptoed over to look at the controls which operated the loading bay shutter.

Fergus's natural instinct was to try to get help from outside as soon as possible but his hopes of a sharp exit were dashed almost immediately. Instead of the shutter door having a simple up and down button, there was a much more complicated keypad that needed a combination number to activate it. With a sinking feeling Fergus realized that there was going to be no quick escape, and that if he was to take any action it would have to be in the other direction, further into the building.

The loading bay had little to offer other than more smelly white containers, so with his heart starting to beat faster Fergus took a deep breath and approached the door that Beanface had taken Murdo through a few minutes before. Praying that there would be no squeaky hinges, Fergus eased the door open as carefully as he could, managing to do so without a sound. He listened for a few moments as he held the door ajar, making sure that there was no one in the corridor beyond.

As he was about to go further, Fergus once again had the momentary feeling that there was something else nearby, just as he had when he looked out into the yard a few minutes before. This time he thought he heard the rub of a plastic box on the concrete floor, but having opened the door he couldn't waste time looking back. Steeling himself for whatever was to come, he headed through the door and let it close again quietly behind him.

Fergus found himself in a brightly-lit corridor and was immediately faced with a choice of turning left or right. He had no way of knowing which way Beanface and Murdo had gone, but from Jessie's description of the shop, his sense of direction told him that the left-hand option led towards the back of the fishshop and to Raeburn Place, with Stein's office nearby. Fergus didn't need long to realize that if he suddenly appeared by Beetroot's side behind the fish counter then his investigations would be over very quickly. Turning right instead, he crept as silently as he could along the straight corridor, which ended in the distance at another door with a large "Caution" sign on it.

Feeling increasingly nervous but convinced that this was the right direction to go in, Fergus carefully opened that door, leaning around it to peer into the gloom. As he took a step through it, he suddenly found that there was nothing for him to stand on. The door swung fully open and the ground seemed to disappear beneath his feet. Fergus was suddenly hanging onto the door handle with his feet flailing beneath him in the air.

As he swung on the door, his mind flashing, the rucksack seeming even more in the way and his legs flapping uselessly below him, he caught a glimpse of a steep metal ladder which dropped away immediately below the door frame. The door swung closed, Fergus waggled his feet, just managing to make contact with the ladder. Then grabbing one of the rungs with one hand, he let go of the door handle, letting the door close with a heavy metallic ring. As Fergus clung shaking to the ladder, his pulse thumping and breathing fast, he realized that the sound of the door closing was the noise that he had heard in the distance as Murdo and Beanface had disappeared moments before. At least he now knew that he was going in the right direction to track them down, even if he had nearly broken his neck in the process. He finally got his racing heart back under control. "Now I see what they mean by 'Caution,'" he thought wryly.

With a deep breath and firmly blanking out any thought of Jessie telling him to go no further on any account, he began to descend the metal ladder as quietly as he could, a dull tapping ring sounding as he placed each foot.

He felt a surge of relief as his feet found a hard floor once again and he took the chance to look around. Rather than the brightly lit carpeted corridor, which led him to the "Caution" door, Fergus now found himself in a dark passageway with an old flagstone floor and walls of rough stone. Every few metres there were basic lamps that gave off a dingy glow and provided just enough light to get from one to the next without disappearing into darkness between them.

As Fergus began to creep his way along the passageway, all of his senses alert to the possibility of both hearing or making any noise, he began to pick out a pattern of high archways in the ancient stone walls. The gap underneath each one was like a dark cave, the limit of which couldn't be seen. It slowly dawned on Fergus where he was. "The vaults," he said quietly to himself taking in the fact that he was now looking at a hundred years of engineering history propping up a busy Raeburn Place a few metres above his head. Fergus ran his hands along the rough stone. Parts of the corridor not only looked like they were a century old but had a musty smell that seemed to date back just as far. Fergus shivered. The temperature had dropped since he had come below ground and as he glanced at the temperature readout on his DataBoy he saw it reduce by two degrees.

Fergus might have imagined that the further he went into the vaults, the more he would go back in time. But although the start of the corridor had seemed like stepping into the past, he soon began to realize that he was actually looking at a mixture of the past and the future. He had only gone the distance of about a dozen lamps along the passageway when he came upon the first of a number of polished steel doors fitting neatly into the vaulted arches. Each had a numbered keypad on the wall beside it.

The first two doors were unmarked. Fergus listened at them but could hear nothing. The third door had a small square glass window in it and Fergus stood on tiptoe to peer through, dimly making out some straight shapes through the glass in the darkened room.

"Bunk beds?" he whispered to himself in a puzzled voice. The memory of Cogs not going home during one of the days of the stakeout came back to him and Fergus wondered if this room provided an answer to that mystery.

His mind began to race as he suddenly realized that they might well have misjudged the scale of whatever operation was going on. They had only really seen Cogs, Beetroot, Beanface, Stein and MM but what if they were only the visible side of the team? This room contained three sets of bunkbeds and at a glance, a few of them were being used. This was definitely a bigger operation and again Fergus heard Jessie's voice saying, "Get out now and get some help!"

Fergus finally admitted to himself that she was right and fumbled for her mobile phone, but even before he tried to switch it on he guessed with a sinking heart that there would be a problem. At ten metres underground there was not even the hint of a signal. The old phone lay useless in his hand. Fergus was unable to make contact with anyone outside and was equally untraceable. The only person who knew he was here was Murdo and he was equally far below ground and probably under lock and key into the bargain. With a feeling of impending doom, Fergus reached the conclusion that going further into the vaults was not a good option, but it was the only one that he had.

He took a few more tentative steps along the passageway. The signs on the doors were beginning to give some idea of what the rooms were used for. "Laboratory 1" was empty and dimly lit and Fergus could just make out metal workbenches, kitchen equipment and a giant oven in one corner.

Tiptoeing further Fergus came upon Storeroom A, but peering through the glass panel in the door, he struggled to make anything out in the gloom. Remembering that he was carrying Murdo's rucksack stuffed with equipment, he rummaged for a torch. Through the glass the beam of light picked out large silver drums stamped on the side with "Nine Lives."

Next up was Storeroom B where the torch revealed boxes filling the room from floor to ceiling. One lying open showed it packed with tins of Nine Lives catfood. Fergus presumed that the production and storage facility that seemed to be housed in the vaults had been a busy place in the lead-up to the launch of the new product. He could hear Gill Hall's voice in his head, though, saying "People are allowed to have businesses that make and sell cat food, Fergus. There's nothing wrong in that."

Fergus knew that he had to find out more and it was only by going further into the vaults that he would do so. He continued along the passageway until it turned sharply left and eased himself around the corner, fearful that he might bump into someone at any moment. The cold air of the vaults was beginning to make him shiver and he now had to go some distance before he reached the next door. He began to wonder if there was a much bigger room behind the rough stone wall than those he had seen so far.

When he eventually reached a door, excitement and disappointment surged through him in equal measure. "The Chamber!" Fergus said to himself, reading the nameplate and remembering this name from a file that Jessie had seen in Stein's desk. However this time there was no glass panel and no way of seeing what was behind the door. Whatever took place in the Chamber remained tantalizingly out of reach. Fergus was convinced that this was a room with more answers than storerooms, laboratories and bunk-bedrooms had to offer and he loitered outside as he tried to work out what to do next. He also wasn't in a hurry to go much further as he didn't like the way that the corridor headed off into even murkier darkness beyond this point.

Fergus looked more closely at the door to the Chamber. The most obvious features were the sign saying "Authorized

Personnel Only" and a large digital clock above the door. Fergus automatically checked and set his DataBoy to the time shown. To one side of the door were temperature and humidity gauges and a numbered keypad. It had a digital readout saying "access code required for entry."

Fergus felt sure that this was the place to be but he didn't know what numbers he needed to get in, let alone how many were in the sequence or what order they should be pressed in.

And then it came back to him. The access code that Murdo had read out in the van. Could that have been Beanface's reminder to himself to get into this room? Surely Beanface would be "authorized personnel?" Fergus knew immediately that there was only one way to find out and scrolled through the options on his DataBoy to recall the number he had entered only an hour before. Checking the passageway to make sure that he was still alone, he put his ear to the door to be certain that he wasn't going to walk in to a roomful of people. Everything was quiet and so with a silent apology to Jessie for going even further into places that he shouldn't, Fergus pressed 5, 1, 3, 2, 9 and a button marked "Enter Code."

Just as he pressed the handle and the door began to open, Fergus heard a distant thud back along the passageway. It sounded as thought the door at the top of the metal ladder had swung closed again. Realizing that this meant that someone could be heading his way within a minute, Fergus pushed the door of the Chamber open just far enough to slip through before closing it softly again behind him.

Once inside, he was bathed in a dull blue glow. He blinked as his eyes adapted not just to the light, but to the sight that greeted him. In front of him all around the walls, from floor to ceiling and stretching far off into the distance, was row upon row upon row of glass boxes. His first thought was that the walls were stacked high with fish tanks, each with wires and tubes coming out of them. It had never really occurred to Fergus that the cats which Murdo had compiled information on, were only a small proportion of those that had disappeared. He now faced the shock that the forty-four missing cats that they knew of were just the tip of the iceberg. As his eyes adjusted to the gloom he gazed at hundreds of boxes. Each one held a sleeping cat.

14. The Chamber

Fergus moved towards the wall of glass boxes as if hypnotized, drawn closer by the sight of the cats. There were more cats here in one place than he had seen in the whole of his life. Fergus let his gaze run as far as he could see into the dimly-lit room. At a rough guess there must have been four or five hundred cats of all shapes and sizes, from scarred city tomcats to fluffy suburban Persians. At first glance it appeared like an enormous museum display of stuffed animals but as he moved closer he could see slight movements as each cat breathed in its sleep. Peering more closely at the containers Fergus saw that each one had a simple label with a serial number and a location. 0014 Edinburgh, 0036 Newcastle, 0045 Aberdeen. Fergus's mind whirled. In just a few metres of wallspace he could see about seven different cities. Their investigation wasn't just about a few cats in Comely Bank. It was about all of the numbers and cities he had seen on the clipboard in the loading bay.

Examining the boxes that the cats were contained in, Fergus could see that each had a tiny control panel with display gauges for temperature, nutrients and oxygen levels, while a flickering red number showed the cats' steady pulse rates. Tubes reached from feeding bowls in each glass box down to drums of Nine Lives food stored at ground level, exactly like the ones that Fergus had seen in the laboratories next door. More gauges suggested that the cats' sleeping, waking and feeding patterns were being carefully regulated.

Looking further into the Chamber, Fergus also now

noticed what looked like a control console for the whole room. It was the size of two large desks and had dials, lights and sliding knobs that seemed to play a part in maintaining stable conditions in the room. There was little sound other than an occasional bleep from some of the electronic equipment which drew Fergus's attention to the only other structure in the room, a huge unit the size of a giant telephone box in the middle of the floor. A plaque at the top read "The Timebank." Beside it a large digital clock showed hours, minutes and seconds in red digits. Below this on each of the four sides of the Timebank were numbered panels the size of postcards. Fergus quickly made the link that the numbers on each panel matched every cat's container. On every little panel was a tiny digital clock counting down through days, hours, minutes and seconds, each readout at a different stage. Under each clock in small letters it read "Time Remaining to Preference Transfer Completion."

Fergus weighed up everything that he seen so far and felt it all begin to fall into place. He was looking at hundreds of cats, each being controlled and fed for a set length of time until they had developed a liking for Nine Lives, without even realizing they'd been eating it.

It was like a breathtaking scene from a science fiction film and once again Fergus could see that in future Murdo's crazier suggestions would merit serious discussion.

Thoughts flashed through Fergus's mind about what he could do. He decided that he couldn't try to free the cats. Although the cats had been stolen, it at least appeared that they were alive and relatively comfortable and he didn't want to disrupt that.

Fergus knew that somehow he needed to get a message above ground to let people know that this was where the cats were and then let the experts deal with it.

Looking around the Chamber again at the scale of

the scene, he knew how far-fetched it would sound if he tried to describe it. He decided that he needed proof so he delved into the rucksack and worked his way through the equipment until he found Murdo's digital camera. A quick glance showed him that there were very few buttons to manage and that the flash was automatic. Fergus lined up a shot that would include the control console and the banks of glass cases along the walls in the background. He steadied himself and prepared to take a picture. "Right, Exhibit A," he said to himself.

Just as he pressed the button there was a brief thought in his head that this maybe wasn't such a good idea. As soon as he took the picture he realized why. The flash exploded into the gloom and sirens immediately began blaring, echoing around the huge Chamber. The needle gauges on the console bounced towards a threatening-looking danger zone and an angry red light flashed under a glass panel saying "SYSTEM ALERT." Before he could even think of an escape plan the door burst open and a man who Fergus recognized as Cogs ran in. He was brought up short by the sight of Fergus but gathered himself together quickly.

"What did you do?" he snapped, his voice cutting through the piercing noise of the siren.

Fergus was surprised that the first question wasn't about him or why he was there. He was sure they wouldn't be far behind but for the meantime the man obviously just wanted to deal with the emergency.

"What did you do?" Cogs rattled out the question again and this time grabbed Fergus's arm as he did so.

"I took a photo," Fergus said meekly holding up the camera. For a moment Cogs looked confused. "It flashed," Fergus added.

Cogs visibly relaxed with the news that Fergus hadn't done any more damage than that. He grabbed the camera from Fergus and turned to the control console before punching a series of buttons. The siren immediately cut off and faded to an echo around the room. The needles on the gauges shrank back out of the danger zone and the lights on the panel flickered for a last time and then stopped flashing.

Cogs turned to look at Fergus and at the same time picked up a phone connected to the console.

"It's Lomax," he said. "We have ... we have an intruder in the Chamber. The boss should come down."

Fergus was bundled roughly into a swivel chair beside the control console. Cogs then thought better of his decision and wheeled the chair some distance away as if expecting that Fergus would dive towards the buttons and switches if he sat anywhere near them.

After the shock of setting off the siren, Fergus sank into a low mood as he realized that he had gone from potential rescuer to just another captive by clicking a camera button.

The longer he sat there, however, he decided that he still had to make the most of the situation. He imagined that he had Jessie and Murdo for company and that the three of them were working out what to do next. Jessie, he decided would have switched on her beady eyes in order to take in some of the details of the Chamber. Fergus started counting the cat containers, but as his eyes drifted along the wall they began to blur into one another and he lost count at 143.

Next he turned his attention to the console but found that he had been wheeled too far away from it to make sense of the buttons and switches or to see what the writing said. As Cogs was now seated at the console he was also blocking some of it from view and any time that he wasn't adjusting switches and knobs, he seemed to spend turning to give Fergus a hard stare.

Fergus then looked at possible escape routes, but the

only route out seemed to be the door that he had entered through and what appeared to be a sliding door with a touch pad on another wall, although there was no indication of where it led.

Fergus glanced at his watch to check on how long he had been underground but stopped in puzzlement. The DataBoy was showing an earlier time than it had when the boys were back at the loading bay. It had gone backwards. Fergus gazed around the room once again. It was as if the Chamber itself was having an effect on the watch. As he watched, the bleep sounded again as the readouts on each panel of the Timebank counted down another thirty seconds and Fergus made another connection. "The bleep from the tape," he said quietly to himself.

It was then that he noticed a small plate attached to the Timebank. "Warning — timepieces may be affected. Please reset with corridor clock on departing the Chamber."

Fergus looked up into the gloom towards the ceiling. In the middle there was a dark shaft like a wide chimney disappearing further upwards and out of sight. It dawned on him that he was sitting directly underneath the manhole cover on Comely Bank Avenue. They had nearly looked down on the Chamber right at the start of their investigation. "So you've found our little animal sanctuary."

Fergus spun round to find Davidson Stein standing by the control console. He had entered the room without a sound and he gave an almost imperceptible nod, indicating to Cogs that he was to leave the room. Cogs gave a last malevolent stare at Fergus and pulled the door of the Chamber firmly behind him, leaving Fergus alone with Stein.

Stein walked up to the console and glanced at it. He then surveyed the length of the walls of cat containers as if he were a king looking proudly over his kingdom. He turned to Fergus and spoke quietly but firmly.

"You are just a little too inquisitive for my liking," said Stein. "You are on private property and you have no right to be here."

"These cats are private property, you have no right to have them here," said Fergus sounding braver than he felt.

"I have no right? ... I have no right?" said Stein repeating Fergus's words as if weighing each one up individually. "Perhaps not, but I have the means and the ability and I will not be stopped."

"I know exactly what you're doing here," said Fergus.

"Oh yes, I've read all about it in your amusing little book," said Stein picking up Murdo's missing Investigation Diary from the console. "But you see children really shouldn't stray into places like this. Accidents can happen." Stein seemed thoughtful as he said this and looked casually around the room as if he was weighing up possibilities.

"It's not just me that knows," said Fergus boldly, trying desperately to sound as if he was part of some bigger rescue plan.

"Oh you mean your sidekick?" said Stein turning to the console and tapping the large keyboard. On a TV monitor on the wall above it, the image changed from the passageway outside to the inside of a room. Around the walls were cages like the ones in the back of the van and there were worktop benches with straps and wires that Fergus guessed were the right size for restraining cats. In a cage in the corner of the room was Jock. Fergus then gasped as he saw Murdo sitting in what looked like a large dentist's chair which he was firmly strapped into. Both he and Jock appeared to be unconscious. At least that was the explanation that Fergus tried to keep in his mind.

"There are others who know," Fergus steeling himself.

"Ah yes, the old lady ... Mrs. ... what shall we call her? Mrs. Sprockett-Jenkins? Well, I can't imagine she's exactly given her approval for you to poke around here, but even if she has done, I'll be taking some steps to take care of her. Terrible how old people can be susceptible to nasty falls, isn't it?"

Fergus felt the heat rise within him. He wanted to say, "You couldn't" or "You wouldn't" but knew that Stein would simply throw those statements right back at him. He was now in full flow.

"Yes, I don't think you can pretend that anyone else knows. I imagine you've been quite happy having your own little secret mystery games to play. I can't imagine it would have gone down too well at home if you'd told your mother that you were planning to break into one of the local shops."

"You are a cat thief and you will be found out," said Fergus trying desperately to sound confident but knowing that Stein had the upper hand.

"And you are currently breaking and entering on private property and I may just have to take appropriate action to defend myself," Stein retorted.

"But people will notice that Murdo and I have disappeared later today," said Fergus.

Stein continued to scan the control console and survey the Chamber seeming not to register Fergus's comment.

"Do I look concerned about that, Fergus?" asked Stein, suddenly turning to face Fergus with a manic grin on his face.

"WELL DO I?" he bellowed, suddenly leaning into Fergus's face and shouting at full volume.

Fergus pulled as sharply backwards as the chair would allow.

"This is *not* someone to get on the wrong side of," raced through Fergus's mind. "Too late!" he could hear Murdo saying as he imagined having the conversation aloud with his friend.

"Don't you wonder why I'm not worried?" continued Stein now moving around behind Fergus, bending low and keeping his voice quiet and close. Fergus could feel Stein's breath on his ear. "You're not going to disappear for long. You'll be back home very soon and so will your friend. You know you really should try to enjoy this bit of the day as much as you can because in a few hours I'm afraid you won't remember any of it."

Fergus's mind started racing. What was Stein's plan? It suddenly seemed that there could be whole filing cabinets of vital information that were missing from Murdo's Incident Room. They really didn't know what was happening in the vaults below Raeburn Place.

"Allow me to show you something," Stein said with a leering smile as he headed back to the console and punched a few buttons.

The image of Murdo tied to the seat re-appeared. Stein continued to attack the buttons on the console with glee and the camera that was focused on Murdo zoomed in. The whole scene with the dentist's chair looked hazily familiar and Fergus forced his brain to try to retrieve where he had seen it before. The screen showed that there were leads attached to the helmet that Murdo was wearing, which looped away from the chair and connected to another console. Stein made more adjustments and the image changed to show the console's gauges. Fergus stared and tried to focus on what the screen showed. There was a digital readout with a timeline that was creeping slowly along. He looked at Stein who grinned back and nodded to him, encouraging him to look again. The timeline said that it was sixty-seven per cent complete and underneath it said "Recall Processor."

A cold feeling crept over Fergus and he froze. The Recall Processor. MM's book.

Fergus began to speak again but found that his voice sounded strangely thin and quiet. "You've been scrubbing bits of cats' memories. That's how you're doing it. Get rid of their memories of the tastes that they like and start them afresh with your own rotten recipes. Then your cat food will be the only thing they'll eat."

"Ah, the boy genius does it again," declared Stein. "Yes I can see now. You're the brains and he's the enthusiasm," nodding towards the screen which showed an unconscious Murdo.

Fergus looked back at the screen. The dentist's chair. The illustration from MM's book came back to him. "You're going to scrub our memories too?" whispered Fergus in shock under his breath.

"Correct again. You see we can identify the most freshly used bits of your memory. That's why I suggest you enjoy these last few hours because I'm afraid in terms of remembering it, it will be a case of here today and gone tomorrow. I'll be the only one with happy memories of the delightful time we've spent together. Now you really must excuse me for the moment as I have some business to attend to. The important launch of the country's newest and soon-to-be most popular and fastest-selling cat food is only days away you know!"

With that Stein strode forward to Fergus and, before he knew what had happened, had handcuffed him to the arm of the seat.

"Don't stray too far!" said Stein smirking at Fergus before turning and striding out of the Chamber.

The room fell silent and Fergus was alone again in the eerie blue glow. He pulled at the handcuffs only to find that there was little room for manoeuvre and no chance of getting out of them. He tried to relax and told himself that spending time thinking was the best thing he could do in the circumstances. His mind whizzed through all the things he had to do. He had to get those electrodes off Murdo who might already be missing chunks of his memory. He had to warn Jessie before Stein sent anyone to get her. He had to get that photo of the Chamber to the outside world yet here he was, handcuffed, with a deranged fishmonger intent on domination of the world of catfood.

Fergus glanced up at the monitor again. The screen that had shown Murdo was flicking through images from four cameras in sequence. Fergus concentrated on trying to see what situation his friend was in. The scenes changed between a view of Murdo in the chair, the gauges of the console that he was connected to, a sliding door in the wall similar to the one in the Chamber and a floor level view that allowed him to see Jock's little body taking short shallow breaths in his cage. As the monitor flicked through each scene, Fergus was able to predict what would come next. There was little change each time they reappeared other than the digital readout on the control panel counting upwards ominously. It now showed that it was eighty-two per cent complete. Murdo was minutes away from forgetting the last few hours.

Fergus closed his eyes with a heavy sigh and a feeling of doom just as a new image appeared on the screen. He blinked open again in an instant. The monitor continued to change in sequence and Fergus watched in amazement as a figure in a hooded top and jeans appeared, creeping into the room where Murdo sat unconscious in the chair.

Fergus realized that perhaps he had been right. There had been someone else both outside and then inside the loading bay, and they were in the vaults right now. What's more it looked like they could be a useful ally. They were certainly tiptoeing around as if they weren't supposed to be here.

He watched the person move towards Murdo and lean in, seemingly to check on how he was and on what the machine was doing that he was connected to. The screens continued to flick through, giving Fergus views of the person from the top of their hooded head to a full-length shot but their identity remained a mystery.

With the timeline now showing ninety per cent, Fergus wanted to shout instructions to the silent screen and words of encouragement to the mysterious helper but he knew that this would be futile. He didn't even know what part of the building they were in.

The mysterious person bent in concentration at the console as if trying to work out what it did and what to do next. The readout was now up to ninety-six per cent complete and Murdo was seconds away from forgetting everything that had taken place in the recent past when Fergus watched the hooded figure hit a button which read "Process Cancellation."

Fergus exhaled. He hadn't even realized that he had been holding his breath as the timeline moved so close to the end.

The figure now moved over to the cage that Jock was in. From what Fergus could make out, Jock was semi-conscious but made a half attempt to sniff at the person despite his sleep-induced state. Suddenly Fergus watched and heard Jock bark at the same time before the little dog slipped back into unconsciousness.

With the sound of Jock's bark so close by, Fergus realized that the room he was looking at on the monitor must be next door. The sliding door on the screen must be connected to the one he was sitting close to.

"Of course," he thought. "Deal with the cats memories in one room and then bring them next door to the Chamber to feed them!"

"In here! In here!" he shouted spontaneously. The figure on the monitor froze and then turned to the sliding door, hitting a touch pad to one side. Fergus saw on the screen and in front of him at the same time, the door in the Chamber wall sliding back to reveal the person who had just saved Murdo.

"All right, Dr. Watson?" said Murdo's sister, Heather.

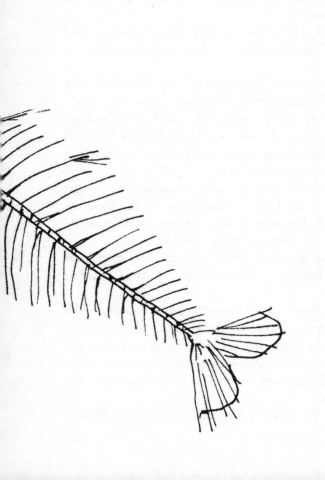

15. Revelations

Fergus felt his jaw drop uncontrollably.

"Wha ... wha ... how ... wha ...?"

"No time to explain," said Heather briskly heading over to look at the handcuffs restraining Fergus. "That mad shop manager could be back at any time."

Heather's prediction was spot on. As she bent to look at Fergus's hands the main door to the Chamber opened and Stein strode in. He looked momentarily amazed to see Heather and annoyed to see the sliding door in the wall open but he recovered his composure quickly.

"Ah, another intruder," he said calmly. "Well, do join the queue. Your friends are just in front of you for a relaxing time in our special chair set aside for unexpected guests." Stein smiled and gestured next door like a deranged waiter ready to show them to their seats.

"You might as well stop all of this now," said Heather now standing behind Fergus's chair. "I've called for help."

"Oh, I hardly think so," said Stein. "I've already been through that somewhat unbelievable scenario with your accomplice here."

Fergus realized that he didn't know if Heather was telling the truth or just bravely bluffing. She had sounded convincing to him but he couldn't really imagine what form help was going to arrive in. He didn't even know how Heather had got involved.

A scraping noise from far above their heads broke his thoughts and at the same time a shaft of light burst downwards into the Chamber, hitting the floor like a spotlight. Immediately the delicate conditions of the Chamber were disrupted again by light, the ear-splitting siren began to sound for the second time in fifteen minutes. Instinctively Fergus, Heather and Stein looked up to find a dark shape hurtling towards them. Fergus realized in an instant that the circle of light that had appeared high above them came from the opening of the manhole cover. At the same time Stein realized that whatever was descending so rapidly was heading straight for him. He dived to one side to get out of the way and landed in a heap on the floor near to the control console as the siren wailed on.

At the last second there was a whizzing sound of glove on rope as the abseiling figure zipped down the last few feet of the long drop from the opening above and hit the floor in a hard but controlled landing.

"Oof! ... I think I'm too old for this," muttered the figure as it turned around.

Fergus's jaw dropped for the second time in two minutes as he first saw a hint of pink cardigan and then saw Jessie gathering herself together. Relief flooded through him for a second until with a panic he cried, "Watch out, Jessie!"

Stein had launched himself from the floor with a snarl to attack this latest intruder but Jessie was seemingly still gathering herself together and checking that she was in one piece.

However, as Stein dived for her, Jessie swivelled, dipped low on one side and extended her right leg fully upwards, catching him perfectly on the chin. He was thrown back with the force of the unexpected karate kick and smashed back into the control console. Lights flashed uncontrollably and the siren volume increased. Stein shook his head to clear it. He looked up with a venomous stare and with a roar leapt up again with his arms outstretched, his fingers hooked like claws as he dived for Jessie's throat. Jessie neatly sidestepped him and as he flew past her she brought her elbow down vertically between his shoulder blades.

"Ouch," said Jessie rubbing her elbow as Stein crumpled to the floor groaning and only semi-conscious. "Now then," she said heading for Stein and briskly checking his pockets. Moments later she had produced a set of keys, freed Fergus and transferred the handcuffs to connect Stein firmly to a pipe running along the bottom of the wall. "That should prevent you hurting yourself again," Jessie said in a kindly voice to a barely conscious Stein. Meanwhile, Fergus hurried over to the control console, spotted an "override alarm" button and returned the room to silence.

He then sprinted through to the other room where Murdo was groggily coming back to life in the dentist's chair.

"What's happening? ... No fillings today? Great ... Fergus what are you doing here? ... Why have I got a helmet on?"

"What did we do this morning, Murdo?" asked Fergus, desperate to check that his friend was all right as he scanned the equipment surrounding him.

"This morning? This morning? Er ... mmm ... not sure really," replied Murdo vaguely, clambering out of the chair.

"The van?" said Fergus hopefully.

"What van? Oh ... Yes ... yes ... yes. The van, the cameras, the five buttons ... Jock! Where's Jock?!"

"Right here, right here, don't worry, I think he's okay," said Fergus unlatching the cage containing the little dog and reaching in to feel that he was warm and breathing. He left the door open so that Jock could get out whenever he woke and turned to Murdo, "Come on through. Wait till you see what's next door!"

Murdo followed Fergus through the door to the Chamber and stood open-mouthed at the sight of so many cats. He looked doubly shocked to find Jessie there and when he looked beyond her to find Stein handcuffed and his sister standing smiling at him, he was, for once, utterly speechless.

"Right, now that we seem to have things in order I have a bone, in fact several bones to pick with you boys," said Jessie looking sterner than they had ever seen her. "I told you very clearly not to do anything silly and you promised that you wouldn't."

"Erm ... I planned to, but I changed my mind," said Fergus looking away and without any good excuse. "I thought you'd gone away," he said desperately trying to change the subject and keen to piece the missing bits of the story together.

"I planned to, but I changed my mind too," said Jessie. "Fifteen minutes ago I heard that alarm go off when I was loading my bags into my friend's car."

"That must have been when I set it off with the camera," said Fergus.

"At the same time," she continued, "I got a text from Heather saying that you had just gone into The Chamber and set off an alarm. I realized that I was right above you so I decided it was time to blow the dust off my old climbing rope and attach it from the car to the manhole cover to speed things up a bit."

"Wait a minute!" exploded Murdo now fully wakened and with no apparent memory problems. "You got a text from Heather?! What do you mean 'a text from Heather?'" Murdo was gradually processing information but could not comprehend how his sister was involved in his own investigation without him knowing.

"Well, it was you boys who put me in touch with her

without realizing it. You had been texting her from my old phone before I had," said Jessie looking pointedly at Murdo who flushed red. "After the stakeout we worked out who each other was and we've been in touch ever since. I know you boys well enough to know that you aren't the most obedient at times and can take matters into your own hands, so Heather was happy to become my back-up plan. I guessed as soon as you both left my flat that you would head straight here, so I immediately recruited her to follow you and keep me up to date with what was happening."

Murdo looked flabbergasted and extremely irritated that his sister had been spying on him.

"You really need to thank her," said Jessie reprovingly. "Without her you could have forgotten about everything that happened down here by the looks of things," she said with a glance at the next-door room.

Fergus noticed that Heather didn't look at all smug, as he would have expected her to be in this situation. In fact she looked pleased to be in on the act and didn't appear to be about to claim the glory.

"You two have been pretty amazing uncovering all of this," she said looking around the Chamber and through to the dentist's chair in the next room.

"Are you feeling all right?" said Murdo, now getting even more confused that his sister was saying something nice to him.

"Murdo, I'm sorry if I've given you a hard time. You can be an annoying little brother but I'm beginning to see that you do have your talents. Without you these cats would all be eating Stein's cat food without even knowing what had happened to them."

"Well," said Murdo blushing, "it's been an interesting investigation. When I think back to the early days when I started off ..."

"Save it Sherlock, I'm not *that* interested," said Heather.

"Hallo down there. Is that Mrs. Jenkins? Are you all right?"

The group all looked up to see a head silhouetted in the circle of light above them.

"Ah good," said Jessie. "I called Gill Hall just before I headed down to join you. She didn't seem too keen on my intentions, but I said that there was no time to lose."

"Yes dear," called Jessie upwards. "We're all perfectly fine, but I think that you should join us here as soon as possible. I'm afraid we might just have added rather a lot to your 'To Do' list for today."

Within a minute, Gill Hall and two other police officers had unrolled a steel ladder and descended into the Chamber.

"I don't fancy the way you came down," said Gill looking at Jessie's ropes before turning to survey the scene in the Chamber and the slumped figure of Stein. He still seemed unsure which bit of his body hurt most, let alone how he'd managed to be beaten up by an ageing ninja.

Jessie launched into as rapid and as simple an explanation as she could, with the boys chipping in some additional facts.

"Right," said Gill to the other officers. "Call for more back-up and then arrest anyone else in the building on suspicion of involvement in theft. The multiple thefts of a few hundred cats by the looks of things. Also I want an arrest warrant issued for Maxine McDermott."

"Green Mazda, registration number MM2," chipped in Fergus.

"You'll find a photo of her on the desk in the office upstairs if you want something to identify her with," said Jessie looking at Stein with a grin.

At that moment Jock wobbled over towards them. Murdo bent to check him out. The little dog looked very woozy but immediately licked Murdo on both cheeks.

"Well he's not forgotten how to do that at least!" said Fergus.

Over by the wall, Stein had gathered himself together although he was still a far cry from the smooth-suited manager they had seen cruising in and out of the shop during the stakeout. Fergus noticed, however, that he seemed to have retained some of his superior air and there was still a hint of his old sneering smile. Eventually Stein couldn't hold himself back from speaking.

"You think you're so clever don't you, but you've not worked it all out you know. You're missing someone. In fact you're missing the main man!"

"What do you mean?" said Fergus.

"It doesn't just stop with me you know. I can exclusively reveal that you still don't know all the facts, but I would be happy to supply them ... in return for some acknowledgement of how helpful I've been." Stein seemed happy to be in a bargaining position as he spoke to the group.

"Stein, you snivelling coward!"

The voice echoed around the room taking them all completely by surprise.

Only Stein sat with a smirk on his face. "If they get me I'm making damn sure they get you too," he shouted backed at the voice, seemingly speaking into thin air.

"You pathetic specimen." It was the voice again. "I should have known that you would blow it."

Fergus knew the voice was familiar but couldn't initially place it or tell where it was coming from.

Jessie spoke next, head cocked to one side as if tuning her ear into whoever they were listening to.

"Bob Crockett?"

Stein smiled in silent satisfaction.

"Yes, Bob Crockett," snapped the voice, "and don't give me any of that 'I'd have thought better of you' rubbish."

"Now, now, temper, temper," said Jessie.

Fergus could picture the bald clock shop owner, his eyes almost popping through his glasses, given how angry he sounded.

"Where is he speaking from?" asked Heather turning slowly around and trying to trace the source of the voice.

"His grandfather's lair, deep in the vaults," said Stein.

"Stein, you scumbag, you maggot, you turncoat!" screeched Crockett's voice.

But Stein carried on regardless. "There's a bizarre system of tubes that allows him to speak into any of the vaults. Another of his grandfather's great inventions that never quite saw the light of day. Although you'll find that some of them have had their uses recently."

Everyone looked blankly at Stein until Fergus broke the silence. "The van!"

"Ah yes, the van ..." said Stein.

"What about the van?" asked Murdo.

"Do you remember when Crockett told us about a few of his grandfather's inventions?" said Fergus.

"Yeah, what was there again?" said Murdo screwing up his face to remember. "Spring-loaded bookends and a marmalade dispensing gun?"

"The telescopic table leg?" offered Jessie.

"And a vibrating mixing bowl," said Fergus.

"So where does the van fit in?" asked Gill Hall.

"Well if you look underneath, those gadgets are all used in some form or other to catch cats. The table legs drop down to form the Capture Plate, the dispensing gun fires fish pellets, there are vibrating plates to stroke the cats and there's a variation on the bookends that form walls to close in and catch them. Would that stand up in court, Gill?" asked Fergus with a grin.

"Oh, I think so. All we need is the accused now," she replied.

"Go to the end of the corridor and lift the trapdoor in the middle of the flagstones," said Stein. "It looks like it's just a small storage space but you can lift another trapdoor in the floor to get into Grandfather Crockett's old workshop. That's where he is."

"STEIN, YOU TRAITOR!" roared Crockett as Gill Hall spoke into her radio and passed instructions to her officers on where to find the irate clock shop owner.

"Well surely that wraps things up now?" said Jessie.

Fergus picked up a folder lying next to the control console and began to flick through the pages one by one. He found that the cats in each numbered case were listed along with the street that they'd been picked up in. This showed that the plan was to release them back home, albeit with a new food fad. Wherever owners had given them collar tags, their names were listed too and Fergus recognized one or two from their file of posters. After running his finger down the list for a few pages he found what he was looking for.

"Number 231, Jessie."

"What dear?"

"Jasper's here. He's number 231."

Jessie gasped and put a hand to her mouth. Everyone watched as she turned away limping over to the wall of glass cases to run her hands along the numbers. After a few seconds of searching she stopped and touched the glass of one of the cases. Behind it her beloved old cat slept, blissfully unaware that he no longer liked peanut butter and marmite on toast.

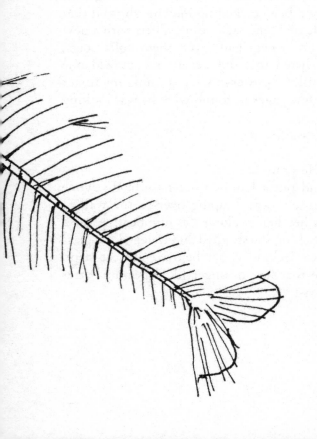

Epilogue

"Well, well, well, what a story," said Jessie folding up the *Evening News* for the third time in ten minutes. Murdo gestured that he would like another read and Fergus looked on even though he had read it from cover to cover a few times already. The local paper had run a special edition on the remarkable story of the lost cats from around the country, the fiendish plans of the fish shop and the investigations that had led to the plot being foiled. There were photos of the boys outside the Incident Room, of Jessie in her white karate gear and a particularly long interview with Beryl Scrimgeour.

The three of them had been passing the paper around for the last hour and a half while they all demolished the biggest plateful of home baking that Jessie had ever produced.

It had taken five days to organize the get-together as both Murdo and Fergus had been grounded.

"Let me get this straight," Murdo had said to his mum. "I spend three months in an extensive investigation, uncover a plot to brainwash a country's cats and lead police to the criminals and I'm not allowed out?"

"That's funny, Murdo," said Mrs. Fraser. "My description reads 'You take unbelievable and unthinking levels of risk, involve other people in them too, lose your dog and nearly your mind,' need I go on?"

Fergus's mum was not far behind with her analysis of what had happened and had even raised an eyebrow at Jessie for leading the boys astray.

But now Jessie and the boys were finally getting the chance to catch up as Jasper slept and Jock sat quietly in opposite corners of Jessie's living room.

Also in the room next to the computer was a huge tower of Nine Lives cat food. Each of the owners of the previously lost cats who had so far been tracked down had been given a large supply for free. This meant that they all had some food that their cats would definitely like while they worked them back to enjoying whatever they used to eat before their time in the Chamber.

"So," said Jessie passing round the cakes again, "the big question is, what are you two going to do with the reward money?"

"I'm going to get a new watch," said Murdo. "There's a closing down sale at Crockett's so I might get a bargain!"

"What about you, Fergus?" asked Jessie.

"I might get a scooter so I can keep up with Murdo!" said Fergus. "But I was also thinking about getting a computer."

Jessie looked away. "Yes, I can see why you would want to get your own and not have to rely on mine anymore."

Fergus noticed that Jessie's voice sounded a bit flat. "Don't worry, Jessie," he said, "I'll still have to come here for computer training."

"And I plan to do visits and spot checks to make sure that your baking standards aren't slipping," added Murdo in a serious tone.

"Oh, good," said Jessie brightening up again. "I'd hate to think that our adventures were ending here."